D1647105

*The Stone That
Never Came Down*

The Stone That Never Came Down

JOHN BRUNNER

NEW ENGLISH LIBRARY
TIMES MIRROR

All of the characters in this book are fictitious, and any resemblance to actual persons, living or dead, is purely coincidental.

First published in the USA by Doubleday & Co., Inc. in 1973
First published in Great Britain by New English Library in 1976
© 1973 by Brunner Fact and Fiction Ltd.

*

FIRST NEL PAPERBACK EDITION MAY 1978

*

NEL Books are published by
New English Library Limited from Barnard's Inn, Holborn, London EC1N 2JR
Made and printed in Great Britain by Hunt Barnard Printing Ltd., Aylesbury, Bucks.

45003294 9

Contents

BOOK ONE

Ascent

Dissidentes Christianorum antistites cum plebe discissa in palatium intromissos, monebat civilius, ut discordiis consopitis, quisque nullo vetante, religioni suae serviret intrepidus. Quod agebat ideo obstinate ut dissensiones augente licentia, non timeret unanimantem postea plebem, nullas infestas hominibus bestias, ut sunt sibi ferales plerique Christianorum expertus.

—Ammianus Marcellinus: *Res Gestae*

I

The morning after it went up . . .

Snow on Chater Street in London's Kentish Town. It was such a hard winter all over Europe that meteorologists were now confidently predicting Britain's first "white Christmas" for many years, in the intervals of disputing learnedly about the effect of high-flying planes, the displacement of jet-streams, and suchlike. In a front-to-back ground-floor room—*the* ground-floor room—at number 25, Malcolm Fry was roused by his bed-side radio.

".\. . and found the bagpipes playing the octopus!" There followed a burst of synthetic-sounding recorded laughter.

—What the hell?

Muzzily, out of the depths of the best sleep he had enjoyed for months.

Then a sycophantic announcer said, "Thank you, Home Secretary, for sharing with our listeners one of your favourite jokes. Tune in at the same time tomorrow, when another distinguished sponsor of the Campaign Against Moral Pollution will prove it doesn't have to be vulgar to be funny. Remember, dirt demeans!"

—Oh. Of course. Radio Free Enterprise. We were making up parodies on the commercials last night. But I feel very strange. I feel . . . How do I feel?

The word came to him, and for a long moment he could not convince himself that it was accurate.

.—Happy.

But what in the world did Malcolm Fry have to be happy about? Unemployed at thirty-five, quite likely unemployable,

in his own profession at any rate; abandoned by his wife, who
had taken the children and the car six months ago; head over
ears in debt that every passing day of inflation worsened . . .
Granted, Ruth had stayed the night, unprecedentedly, and lay
cosily beside him, oblivious to the radio and the time. That
alone, though, could not account for his state of mind, because
the reason why she had stayed . . .

—She was right. I must have been worse than drunk. I must
have been totally, absolutely out of my skull. Just as she said.
I never did a crazier thing in my whole life. Taking a pill from
a stranger in a pub, swallowing it on nothing more than his
say-so! It could have been poison. I think I wanted it to be
poison. I know I was miserable enough.

Although in the upshot . . .

The radio played a snatch of *Land of Hope and Glory*. He
stole a hand out of bedsnug to reduce the volume. It was
dreadfully cold in here. Filtered by the dervishes of the snow,
a street-lamp beam lanced between the curtains and showed
him his breath clouding before his face. The time-switch which
had brought the radio to life also controlled an electric fan-
heater, but the middle element was broken and anyhow the
power was usually browned out nowadays. If only he could
afford to turn on the central heating . . .

Still, it was lovely and warm in the bed, and because the
clock showed only 7:52 he could spare another few minutes
before he roused Ruth. Even if he didn't have a job, she did,
and what was more with the Civil Service, in a department
where unpunctuality counted heavily against her. She had told
him she must wake at eight sharp, which was why he had set
the alarm. Mostly he didn't bother. What did he have to wake
up early for?

So for a while yet he could relish the memory of last night.
Voicelessly moving his lips, he shaped the name Morris, the
stranger, had given to what was in the pill. The capsule, to be
more exact.

"VC!"

And added, *"Wow."*

Some time around midnight they had been debating what the initials might stand for, and after dismissing the obvious possibilities they had dissolved into helpless laughter when Ruth proposed the perfect answer: *vigorous copulation!*

—Oh, fantastic! And if what I'm feeling now is a side-effect, there ought to be more of it about!

The radio said, "And now a summary of the news. Many famous personalities in finance and show business, who thought their wealth would give them immunity to indulge their degenerate lusts, will appear in court this morning following a police raid on a house in London at two A.M.—"

Malcolm started. He almost never listened to Radio Free Enterprise, the London commercial station launched a couple of years ago—not that the BBC was much better these days—but he distinctly recalled that their news bulletins were hourly on the hour.

"The president of the World Bank," the radio said, "is flying to Rome today in a last-ditch attempt to solve the Italian financial crisis. Mobs of unemployed in Turin and Milan—"

—Load-shedding! Cuts the frequency! Of course! Bet a million clocks in London are slow this morning!

But it wasn't that which made him gasp and drive his elbow into Ruth's ribs. At the edge of hearing, against the drone of traffic building up to the regular day-long jam on the nearby motorway—left unfinished when funds ran out, like so much else in contemporary London, so that it terminated in a monstrous bottleneck—a rhythmical sound. He recognised the pattern though he could not make out the words. Many people loudly chanting *That Old-time Religion.*

—And coming closer, too. Damn! Damn!

He scrambled out of bed, seizing a bathrobe, and rushed to the street window. Already there were more noises added to the singing: people shouting encouragement or orders to stuff the row.

"Is it time to get up, darling?" Ruth inquired sleepily. One-eyed, she peered at the clock.

"That's slow," Malcolm grunted, peering discreetly past the

muslin veiling the lower half of the window: ugly, but impera-
tive since he had taken to sleeping down here. Stage by stage
he had had to rent out the house, losing first the children's bed-
rooms, then what had been his and Cathy's, and at last his
cherished study, until this room was his actual home.

"Slow!" Ruth flung back the covers. "I'll have to run!"

He glanced at her. For a fleeting instant he relished the
sight of her bare body; older than him by five years, but single
and childless, she had kept her figure and could still wear the
size in clothes she had taken at twenty. Moreover her face was
fascinating: not beautiful because her nose was too sharp and
her mouth too big, but warranted to catch the eye of every
man she passed.

And then he said, "Sorry, Ruth. Run is exactly what you dare
not do."

"What? Why not?" Dressing hastily in her T-shirtlike un-
dervest, bloomers halfway to her knees, a drab navy-blue skirt
and matching shapeless jacket . . .

—Last night I said as I undressed her, "What became of colour in the world?" And she replied, "Fashion, I suppose." But
that can't be right. I recall when Cathy and I first met: her
girl-friends arriving for parties in midwinter, whisking off fog-
damp cloaks to reveal frocks barely more opaque than the
mist outside. And in the daytime brilliant Norwegian tights
that made girls' legs twinkle like a firework display . . . Now
it's brown or black or grey, and worse yet thick and ugly!

Aloud: "Listen. Can't you hear them?"

She cocked her head in a manner that made an almost painfully perfect curve of her sleek dark hair, and turned pale.

"Oh, no! Godheads?"

"I'm afraid so. Since the pay-rise at Rexwell Radio last
month we've been infested. Trust them to go where the pick-
ings are fattest. And not everyone is telling them to shut up,
either. I have noseyparkers for neighbours, you know. I swear
they could tell my lodgers by sight before I could. If they get
wind of you, the shameless hussy who's spent the night with a
married man . . . The godheads around here are worse than

the average run, too. There are a lot of Irish refugees who miss the fighting they enjoyed back home, and their priests are encouraging them to join up with the ordinary godheads. It's supposed to be a way of keeping unemployed men out of trouble. I saw an idiot parson on TV the other day who made it sound as though he was sending his congregation—well, out carol-singing!"

"Finding the note that can shatter glass?" Ruth suggested with the dry wit which had been among the first things to attract him to her. He contrived a smile, but it was skeletal.

"Okay," she said eventually, fully clad now. "I have some Christmas shopping-time I haven't used, so I can risk being late for once . . . Come to think of it, most of us in the office haven't used our shopping-time. What's the point when everything is so expensive? Would it be safe for me to sneak to the bathroom?"

"Yes, of course. So long as you don't let Mary see you." Mary was one of the lodgers; she was devout, spending every evening either praying at home or attending Bible class with a girl-friend, and at weekends went home to her parents. He scarcely knew her, but she did pay regularly. "I'll make some tea."

As she stole into the hallway, he moved towards the far end of the room. When he and Cathy chose the house, they had confidently expected this to be the next district made fashionable by the insane inflation of London house-prices, so they had created an expensive open-plan kitchen/dining/living area out of the original two ground-floor rooms. Instead, there had been a recession. The area was still mostly borderline slum, and no other house in the street had been painted for at least five years.

—An ideal target for godheads, regardless of anything else . . .

But his mood of euphoria, for the time being, was proof against anything.

—So what if I did act crazy yesterday? The whole damned world is going off its rocker. TV news last night: half the blacks in America seem to have declared civil war, half the Georgians in Russia have decided on UDI and they smuggled that film of Tbilisi in flames to the West to prove it. The planet's cracking like the shell of a hard-boiled egg under the hammering of riots, insurgency, brushfire war . . . And these idiots here, our "beloved leaders"! Content to waste two million of the best-trained workers in the world, to let them stay out of work for months on end, when anyone with a grain of sense can see we *need* them because this city's practically collapsing around our ears!

He set the kettle to boil. From overhead came the noise of creaking boards. That was the American, Billy Cohen, preparing to leave for work. Billy was the nicest of his lodgers, far nicer than Mary, or the colourless student Reggie, or Len the middle-aged clerk embittered by divorce ten years ago, ever willing to complain about his wife to anybody who would listen. Billy had a job—lucky devil—at a bookstore in Hampstead. Six foot two and solidly built, he always made the floor complain when he strode across it.

And here was Ruth back again, hastily, like a thief. Saying as she closed the door, "Malcolm, do they—well, do they know who you are?"

"How could they help knowing? My picture was plastered all over the papers, wasn't it? And I'm still a grand scandal in the district—me, the teacher who corrupted innocent kids! So I always have to buy them off, and they're never satisfied with less than a fiver. I can't afford it, but I could even less well afford to have them work the house over. If somebody from my mortgage company found they'd wrecked the place, I'd be done for. Homeless as well as jobless."

Warming the pot, measuring out the tea, he improvised words to fit the distant chanting—not so distant, now; the godhead gang must be almost at the corner of the street.

"Oh, it's good to screw your sister—sorry, I'm a trifle manic this morning—it was good for Cain and Abel, so it's good enough for me! And it's good to screw your daughter, yes it's

good to screw your daughter, it was good for Papa Lot and
so . . ."

The words trailed away as he glanced up and found her
grinning at him.

"Know something?" she said. "About last night?"

"What?"

"It was never so good for me before. Not with anybody. It
was as though you'd climbed inside my head and knew what
I wanted done next before I'd thought of it myself."

"I'm glad," he said. "It was fantastic for me as well. Thank
you."

There was a momentary pause. Then, with a shrug, he
moved towards the door.

"They're coming," he said. "Four of them. I'd better answer
right away, or they'll smash a window or two . . . No, wait a
second." He checked, reaching for the handle. "I can hear Billy
coming down. He has a job and I don't. Let him deal with
them for once!"

He turned back to finish making the tea.

"Malcolm!" Ruth said suddenly.

"Yes?"

"Malcolm, there's thick snow on the ground out there. It's
still falling."

"So?" He was filling the pot in a cloud of steam.

"How the hell do you know there are four godheads on the
way? They aren't singing that I can hear—if they're there at
all!"

On the point of bringing milk from the refrigerator, Malcolm
froze and stared at her.

"That's right! I . . . I don't know. But I'm absolutely certain.
I can even tell that there's one fat and one thin and— Oh, no!
The bloody fool!"

"What is it?"

"Billy! He's arguing with them!"

"I don't hear—" Ruth began, but he had rushed past her and
out into the hallway.

There as predicted was Billy in his shabby red mackinaw

confronting exactly four godheads: all carrying their typical yard-high crosses made of plastic designed to imitate wood with the bark on, all better dressed than he was, in well-tailored coats, fur hats, fur-lined boots. Godheads, it was estimated, had turned begging—or as they termed it, alms-collection—into a multimillion-pound industry these last few years.

And Billy was saying to their leader, a brown-haired brown-eyed man nearly as tall as himself, "Christians, are you?"

The leader took a half-pace back on the snow-slippery step. He said resentfully, "We weren't told this had become a Jewish household!"

—Given Billy's archetypal appearance, hook nose, swarthy complexion, and the rest, that's a reasonable assumption.

But Billy's response was a snort.

"See any mezuzahs on the doorpost, do you? Not that you'd know what the word means! Well, I tell you what!" He dug in the pocket of his jacket and produced a ten-pound note. The eyes of all the godheads bulbed eagerly.

"I'll give you this!" Billy barked. "Provided you can answer me a simple question!"

"Billy!" Malcolm called from the door of his room. "It's okay —leave it. I'll give 'em something."

"What? Oh, morning, Mal. No, this is my treat today! I just want a simple question answered, like I say!" He faced the godheads again.

"You can have this if you name a weapon of modern war that wasn't invented and first used by a Christian country!"

"Oh, no!" Malcolm heard Ruth breathe at his side.

"Come on, come on!" Billy rasped. "Don't bother going back to gunpowder. I know the Chinese got at that first. But I also know you lot were so eager to steal the credit that if you were German you were taught it was invented by *Friar* Berthold Schwartz and if you were English that it was invented by *Friar* Roger Bacon—good churchmen both! *Well?*"

"Billy!" Malcolm advanced into the hallway, careless of how cruel its ice-cold tiles were to his unshod feet.

Baring his teeth, Billy ignored him and stuffed his money back in his pocket.

"Can't answer me, hm? Not surprising! The whole lot is yours, from the hand-grenade to the hydrogen bomb! So stop wasting my time. I have to go to work. And it wouldn't do you any harm to work for a change, instead of sponging off the rest of us who do!"

Roughly he shouldered the leader of the godheads aside.

That was a mistake.

The man lost his footing on the steps and with a yell went sprawling down to street-level, upon which his companions retaliated.

Their crosses made admirable clubs.

II

"Good morning, milady," said Tarquin Drew. "I trust you have heard the good news on the radio?"

"I have indeed, Tarquin," answered Amelia, Lady Washgrave, as she entered her breakfast-room. Snow lay thick on the lawn beyond the floor-to-ceiling windows, but within the air was warm and deliciously scented with Earl Grey tea.

Tarquin was her personal secretary, and she had conceived a considerable affection for him. His father, incredibly, was an uncouth charge-hand in a factory, and salted his conversation with appalling objurgations. Tarquin had managed to live all that down. Granted, some breath of scandal had attached to him at university . . . but "there is more joy in heaven."

Deftly he aided her chair to adopt its correct posture beneath her decently long skirt. She was a perfect model of what, in her view, a respectable widow of forty-eight should look like. It had been at the age she herself had now attained that the late Sir George had succumbed to a heart attack precipitated, no doubt, by excessive dedication to his business interests. She had borne the loss with fortitude, perhaps not unmingled with relief.

"Would you prefer the *Times* or your correspondence first, milady?" Tarquin enquired, turning to the sideboard. And added in a regretful tone, "I'm afraid the newspaper has not accorded the same prominence to the police's raid as did Radio Free Enterprise."

He displayed the headlines to prove his point; they concerned strikers in Glasgow, riots in Italy, and suchlike trivia. Lady Washgrave was unsurprised; it was notorious that the media, including even the august *Times*, were mouthpieces for the international conspiracy of corruption. She waved the paper aside and accepted an inch-thick wad of letters, most of which, she noted with approval, were from local chapters of the Campaign Against Moral Pollution—of which she was executive chairman—and bore the campaign's symbol: a cross-hilted dagger spiking a stylised book, intended to represent morality cleansing the world of trash.

These at least could be trusted to inform her of *important* matters.

"There were also a hundred and eighty Christmas cards," murmured Tarquin. "And—ah—some abusive items which I took the liberty of extracting. For the police."

Lady Washgrave nodded absently, setting aside the topmost letter because, alas, it could not be relied on to generate action. It was a complaint about the theory of evolution being taught "as though it were a proven fact." The second was a different matter, and ought to cost a teacher, perhaps some school governors and very possibly some local councillors their jobs. To think that a woman living openly in sin should be put in charge of hapless infants!

"Mark that one 'urgent'!" she directed. And, on the point of turning to the next, a description of the behaviour of courting couples on a Gloucestershire common, she checked.

"Is there no communication from Brother Bradshaw?"

"No, milady, I'm afraid there isn't."

"How strange!" She drew her brows together. "The Reverend Mr Gebhart assured me that by today at latest we should be told whether he can join our New Year's Crusade. Admittedly he's greatly in demand, but even so . . . Not that I myself entirely approve of the 'hard-sell' approach, you know, but my committee did vote in favour of inviting him, and one must abide by the democratic principle, must one not?"

"I'll attempt to telephone him later," Tarquin promised.

"Yes, please do." And, having taken a bite of the toast which was all she ever ate in the morning, Lady Washgrave sighed, gazing at the snow-covered lawn. "How beautiful it looks!" she murmured. "So—so pure . . . Which reminds me: you did, I trust, instruct the gardeners to drain the pipe leading to the swimming-pool?"

"Of course, milady. A little more tea?"

Detective Chief Inspector David Sawyer composed a signature block at the bottom of his report and rolled it out of the typewriter. It had been a long report. It had been a long job.

"And completely bloody useless," he said.

On the other side of the office Sergeant Brian Epton glanced up from the charge-sheets he was compiling. "What's useless, chief?" he demanded.

"This whole night's work!"

"I wouldn't say that," Epton countered. "Eighteen arrests, and some of them people who make news by catching cold . . . It's going to look good on the crime-sheet, isn't it?"

"Oh, I admit that," Sawyer grunted, rising and crossing the office to look out of the window. In the yard beyond was a car with a dented wing. Yesterday evening it had been driven into a protest meeting of unemployed Italian immigrant workers, and a man had been sent to hospital with two legs broken. Snow was sifting down, fine as sugar from a dredger. A shivering constable was holding a plastic sheet as a kind of awning over the head of one of the forensic people while he examined the damage to the car.

—Another pin for the map . . .

His eyes strayed to the wall where a visual record was kept of unsolved crimes of violence, a big red, black, or yellow pin marking the spot where the incident occurred.

Every day there seemed to be more of them. More often than not there actually were.

—And what was I doing all night? Spoiling someone's party, that's what.

Aloud, though, as he unhooked his coat from the stand by
the door, he merely said to Epton, "See you this evening, then."

"Yes, of course."

High above Lambeth in his council flat, Harry Bott was
woken by the sound of his children shouting in the adjacent
kitchen, and his wife Vera desperately ordering them to shut
up. Blearily he peered at the luminous Jesus clock beside the
bed. It was just past nine, and he'd intended to lie in late today. He hadn't come home until after 3 A.M., having spent
long cold hours sitting in his car. It had not yet started to
snow, but through the cloudless sky the heat of the land was
being broadcast to the stars.

Still, it had all been worth it. Now he knew exactly how he
was going to carry out the job he'd been planning for so long.

—Not this week, though. Not before Christmas. Directly after
would be best, when trade's at its slackest. Anyway, I'll need
help. Someone to drive, someone to stand lookout, someone to
carry heavy crates.

And with the scheme he had lined up, he could rely on recruiting the best talent in the manor.

His good humour drove away his automatic intention to yell
at the kids. Here in a high-rise block, when the lifts were so
often out of order, where else was there for them to play when
the weather was this bad except at home?

—Of course their cousins . . .

But he was in too good a mood even to feel his regular pang
of jealousy at the luxury his brother-in-law—Vera's brother—
wallowed in, with his big house in Hampstead Garden Suburb
and his two cars and the rest of it. A tickle or two like the one
he was currently planning, and he might be on the way to
similar prosperity.

Humming, he pulled on a dressing-gown and padded into
the kitchen in search of a cup of tea.

"Here's your dad!" Vera exclaimed. "Now you're for it!"

Except for the baby, yelling in his crib, the children fell silent, round-eyed, and she turned from her ironing-board to confront him with tear-stains on her once-pretty face.

"I did try and keep 'em quiet, Harry, honest I did! It's just that I feel so low. I don't have any energy these days." She put her hand on her belly, where three months of pregnancy were just beginning to bulge her cotton overall, and glanced at the picture of the Virgin in its place of honour as though in search of sympathy from another mother. "You know it was like this last time a baby was on the way, and the doctor did say I shouldn't—"

"None of that dirty talk in front of the children!" Harry roared.

The first time the doorbell rang, Valentine Crawford failed to hear it. For one thing, he was trying to fix his baulky oil-heater. On being lit this morning it had uttered foul-smelling smoke, and he had had to let it cool down, take it to bits, and clean the charred wick. Actually he needed a new one, but he couldn't afford it.

And for another thing, he had the radio on. It was all he could offer Toussaint to keep him amused. He had had to turn in the TV last time the rental payments went up.

—Kind of ironical, I guess. Me, a trained TV repairman, and I don't have a set of my own!

But he was out of work, of course. Had been since that horrible, incredible day when the boss had called him in and told him bluntly that he'd have to leave because so many women clients of the firm, on their own during the day, objected to having a black man enter their homes.

—As though I could rape them! Me, a scrawny runt of five foot four! Hell, I couldn't screw them buckra bitches without they help me, start to finish!

He'd tried to lodge a complaint under the Race Relations Act, but nobody was paying much attention to that any more.

The radio was saying, "According to informed sources the chief constable of Glasgow will appeal for the assistance of troops if yesterday's order by the Industrial Relations Court·is not obeyed. Now in its ninth week, the strike at . . ."

Which was not calculated to amuse a six-year-old kid. He wound the knob around in search of music or a comedy show. Meantime the third thing which had prevented him from hearing the bell continued from the bedroom next door, a series of horrible racking coughs.

—If I knew where that she-devil was, I'd . . . !

But he couldn't think of anything bad enough to do to her, the wife who had walked out on him when she grew sick of being mocked and taunted every time she went to the shops with Toussaint.

—Moral, never marry an English girl, not even if you were born on the next street from her home. It oughtn't to make any difference. Hell, I married her because she was pretty and fun to be with and wasn't all made of wood from the waist down like half the English girls. Right from the next damned *street!* But she turned out the same as the rest in the end.

This time the oil-heater lit cleanly and burned with a nice blue flame.

"Okay, son!" he shouted. "It'll be warmer in a minute!"

Whereupon the bell rang a second time, and he answered cautiously, not really expecting that bastard, the local school attendance officer, who had been persecuting him these past few weeks because even with a doctor's certificate he didn't believe Toussaint was too sick to go out, and found Cissy Jones, bright and plump and sixteen and thoughtful, who had brought a bottle of a special cough-mixture her aunt said was very good and should be tried on Toussaint. He liked her, and even before she had measured out a spoonful of the medicine for him he had quietened, as though some of the time he were forcing himself to cough to attract attention.

—But he looks so peaky and he shakes so much . . .

The bell rang again, and here came the rest of them, the rest of the brothers and sisters for whom he ran an informal class in what the authorities at buckra schools didn't want them to find out. A couple of them were playing truant, being not yet past the official leaving-age of fifteen. Some would have liked to stay on at school in spite of all, but hadn't been allowed to. These days it was a common habit to pass over a black kid who talked back to the teachers, and slap on his record a rubber stamp saying INEDUCABLE. And half of them were glad to be out of school, but furious at being out of work as well. Altogether there were ten today.

Five minutes' socialising, and he called for order. From a stack on the mantel Cissy distributed copies of the pamphlet issued by RBR, Radical Black Revival, which they were currently using as a textbook. The pamphlets were numbered because they were precious. One couldn't buy them any more.

Stumbling a little, she read aloud the paragraph at which they had stopped last time.

"'Whereas Sicilian peasants, whose brutal Mafia-dominated culture has ruined their own homeland and who have no less tenuous connection with Britain than the fact that both islands were ruled by Norman bandits some nine centuries ago, are permitted to go and come as they please, blacks from the Commonwealth to whom the British owe an incalculable debt are barred from the nation that grew fat by sucking their ancestors'-blood, or if by some miracle they do achieve entry are constantly at risk of being deported.'"

Valentine interrupted her with a gesture. "Now you all done like I said? You all bought different papers and marked up bits that prove the truth of what the man says there?"

They had, and one by one they read out what they had found. Brooding, he sat and tried to listen, but found he was hearing more clearly the renewed coughs of his half-white son.

III

Brother Bradshaw was in California. His home overlooked a magnificent vista, clear down a long valley, over the silvery mist shrouding Los Angeles, and out to sea. It had been bought before his conversion, when he was one of the world's highest-paid TV stars. If anything, he was handsomer now than he had been at the height of his career; a touch of grey at his temples added distinction, and a little more weight conveyed an impression of trustworthy maturity.

In the old days, the wall of this huge room, which currently was decorated with pictures of him chatting to the Pope, the Cardinal Archbishop of New York, and a great many Just Plain Folks who had Seen the Light because of him, had been covered with a montage of photos showing him in very different postures and many fewer clothes.

"But I don't want to go to England!" he kept insisting, in a voice which annoyance had heightened from its usual resonant baritone towards a querulous tenor. "Don't I have enough to do over here? What with nearly three hundred murders in Greater Los Angeles last month—"

"But this invitation is personal from Lady Washgrave," Don Gebhart insisted. He had said it all before, but he had been a professional evangelist himself until he took over the management of Brother—formerly Bob—Bradshaw, so he was well used to saying the same thing over and over with equal conviction every time. "You know how much weight she swings. Her Campaign Against Moral Pollution has a hundred fifty local chapters. A cabinet minister regularly speaks at her meetings, this guy Charkall-Phelps. And she's batting one-oh-oh in her drive to clean up literature and TV. It's three years since she last had an obscenity verdict overturned on appeal. Nobody monkeys with Lady Washgravel"

"I know!" Bradshaw barked. "I *know!*"

"So why won't you accept?" Gebhart pressed.

Bradshaw didn't answer.

"Listen, Bob," Gebhart said at last. "You never knew me to give you bum advice, did you? Well, what I'm saying is this. You join in her New Year's Crusade, and you'll be on the map for good and all. It would make you—well, it would make you the Billy Graham of the nineteen-eighties!"

More silence. Eventually, with dreadful reluctance, Bradshaw sketched a nod.

"Great!" Gebhart exclaimed. "I'll call her right away—I guess the time is okay in England now—and explain how you want to spend Christmas with your folks, of course, but you'll be right there on December twenty-eighth ready to join in her grand crusade!"

"Damn," muttered Lance-Corporal Dennis Stevens after they had toured the block for the third time. "Nothing else for it, then. You'll have to double-park while I go in alone."

"What else have I been telling you for the past half-hour?" his driver sighed. "Look, lance, the busies aren't going to give *us* a ticket, are they?"

"I suppose not," Stevens admitted, reaching into the back seat of the olive-drab Army car for the cardboard roll containing the posters he was scheduled to deliver at this particular Employment Exchange. How to explain the reason for his unwillingness to enter by himself?

In fact it was very simple. He knew this drab, forbidding building. It was right on his own home patch. He couldn't count how many hours he had wasted waiting here for the chance of work that never materialised, or to claim from grudging clerks the benefit money due to him by law.

So he might very well run into some of his mates here.

And while there was a lot to be said for joining the Army in times of high unemployment—security, technical training, the chance of travel, plenty of sport, and all the rest of it, which had tempted him when he grew bored beyond endurance and certainly had been provided as promised—if it were true, as the headlines on today's *Daily Mirror* claimed, that they were going to send troops to Glasgow and drive the men who'd been on strike these past nine weeks back to work at gunpoint . . . Well, those old mates of his weren't likely to make a soldier very welcome, were they?

"Get a move on, lance!" the driver pleaded.

"Okay, okay!" Tucking the cardboard tube under his arm like a swagger-stick, he crossed the sidewalk with affected boldness, thinking about what the papers had said.

—Never paid too much attention to that old-fashioned stick-in-the-mud I have for a father. But I do believe he's right to say the power to strike is precious. What else are working folk to do if they can't get a decent wage? Bloody fools in Parliament! What do they want, another Ireland on their hands?

As it turned out, he'd worried needlessly; the only person who recognised him was the clerk who had to sign for the recruiting posters, and he offered congratulations on putting up a stripe, having done some Army time himself.

—Thank goodness!

Professor Wilfred Kneller stood gazing down from the window of his office at the sluggish traffic in the street below. He was director of the Gull-Grant Research Institute, which occupied the top floor of a four-storey block on the eastern edge of Soho, premises donated by its founder, who had been a tobacco millionaire with a guilty conscience.

At the time of his appointment eight years ago this had been a lively district, maintaining Soho's long-standing reputation as a centre of night-life—and, of course, prostitution. The recession, however, had taken its toll, and from here he could count half a dozen "to let" signs without craning his neck, testimony to the bankruptcy of restaurants, clubs, and borderline pornography shops.

—How things have changed!

Moreover, during the night, a team of godhead flyposters had been by, and every wall and window in sight was decorated with stickers repeating their current slogan: PUT CHRIST BACK IN YOUR CHRISTMAS!

—That is, apart from the windows that they smashed . . . I wonder how many proprietors went broke because they couldn't afford to insure their plate-glass after the godheads moved in.

"Morning, Wilfred," a voice said from behind him.

"Morning," he grunted in reply. He knew without looking that the speaker was Dr Arthur Randolph, a portly man in his forties—ten years his junior—who, like himself, had been with the Institute since its foundation and who headed one of the two departments it was divided into. Officially his was called Biological, while his colleague Maurice Post's was Organochemical; in practice, particularly since the inception of the VC project, they worked in double harness, sharing funds, lab facilities, and even staff.

—Natural enough. How could you draw a line between living and nonliving where VC is involved?

"Admiring the street decorations, are you?" Randolph went on, walking across the room to join him. "Makes me think of something Maurice once said to me. Maybe to you too, of course."

"What?"

"Oh, he was wondering what society would have been like if we'd socialised cannabis instead of dangerous drugs like alcohol and religion." Randolph chuckled.

Kneller echoed him, but the sound rang hollow, and after a pause Randolph added, "I—uh—I don't suppose there's been any news of him, has there?"

Kneller shook his head. "Arthur, I really do feel we should notify the police, you know. After all, he's been missing since Monday, without a word of explanation or apology."

"I told you before," Randolph said. "If you do that, you risk losing him completely. I can't imagine him being overjoyed, can you, if the police come hunting for him and all he's done is go off quietly by himself to think for a while?"

"You've said that before," Kneller countered stubbornly. "The more time goes by, the less I believe you. It simply isn't *like* Maurice to vanish this way. And nobody knows what's become of him. His landlady hasn't seen hide or hair of him, he hasn't been in touch with his sister at Folkestone, nor with any of his professional colleagues—I mean apart from us. And he doesn't seem to have any private friends to speak of, and he doesn't belong to a church, and . . . I don't see any alternative, really I don't." He tugged at his beard. It was grizzled, and out of style now that razor-sales were back to their previous peak, and several people had said it made him look older than his years. But he had worn it since his mid-twenties, and did not feel inclined to abandon it after more than a quarter-century.

Turning to his desk and gesturing for Randolph to sit down, he pursued, "Tell me candidly, Arthur. Has Maurice done or said anything recently to indicate he might have been—well—overworking?"

With a wave of his hand to acknowledge the tactful equivalent of "had a nervous breakdown", Randolph answered, "I wouldn't have said so. He's always been a funny sort of person, like most confirmed bachelors: a bit irritable, a bit unpredictable . . . Of course, lately he has been very upset about the state of the world. But isn't everybody who bothers to pay attention?"

Kneller gave a wry grimace at that. "I know what you mean! Every damned day the news seems to get worse, doesn't it? You saw that they found a poor devil of a Pakistani beaten to death in a park in Birmingham?"

"I did indeed. And what's more I noticed it in the 'News in Brief' column. We're in a hell of a mess, aren't we, when something like that doesn't make headlines on the front page? But it's not the crimes of violence that scare me. I mean, not the small crimes of violence. I'm worried about the big ones. The kind that could stem from this crisis in Italy, for example."

Kneller shrugged. "What do you expect in a country where it's practically a matter of honour to lie about your income and avoid paying tax? Small wonder they're going broke!"

"That's only the half of it. When the Italians signed the Treaty of Rome they expected to be a net food-exporting country. Within a few years they'd become net importers. So of course they're being bled white by the subsidies given to inefficient farmers in other countries. So are we, come to that. If they do decide to try and pull Italy out of the Common Market, close their frontiers and reimpose protective tariffs . . . Well, the Treaty of Rome is meant to be irrevocable, isn't it?"

"Was it Maurice who sold that line of argument to you?" Kneller demanded.

Randolph looked faintly surprised. "Come to think of it, it must have been. A week or two ago. Why, was he talking about it to you?"

"He did say something about the Third World War being more likely to start that way than by a clash between East and West, or rich and poor. But that's not quite the point. I recall you as having been a fervent pro-Market man ever since we first met."

"Well, I still am!" Randolph declared with a hint of belligerence. "But if the system is this badly mismanaged . . . I do have to confess, though, that the way Maurice put his case made me see things in a different light. But why are you making such a meal of this? That's always been Maurice's special talent: shedding a different light on things."

"I'm not sure," Kneller admitted. "It's just that at the edge of my mind there's something . . . No, I can't pin it down."

"Well, if you really are worried about Maurice," Randolph said, "there's one thing you could do. You're wrong to say we don't know about any of his private friends. Surely his GP is a friend, too. Weren't they at school together?"

Kneller snapped his fingers. "Yes, of course! I should have thought of that before. Isn't his name . . . Hamilton? No,

Campbell, that's it. And his address is bound to be on Maurice's file. I'll send for it."

Hand outstretched towards his desk intercom, he checked. "Arthur, this will probably sound ridiculous, but . . . Look, describe to me what, in your view, Maurice expects VC to do if and when we decide it's safe to administer it to a human subject."

"What?" Randolph stared blankly at him. "Why, you know as well as I do."

"I think I do." Kneller was suddenly very grave. "The stuff's volatile, isn't it?"

"Yes, of course. Or rather, not the stuff itself, but the supportive medium we keep it in. Why?"

"Would it be possible to determine whether there's been a stock loss?"

"A stock loss?" Randolph echoed in perplexity. "Lord, on the molecular level? The quantities we're working with are so damned small! Not a chance."

"Very well, then. Who issues test-samples to the lab technicians and the postgrads—you or Maurice?"

"Maurice. Nine times out of ten at any rate."

"In other words, he's the person who most often opens the sealed vats." Kneller leaned forward earnestly. "And could not the hoped-for effect of VC be described as enabling one to cast fresh light on every single kind of subject?"

There was dead silence for a moment. Randolph turned pale.

"If you mean what I think you mean—"

"You know damned well what I mean!"

"Then you had better get hold of his doctor. Right away!"

Down a half-deserted side-street in Kentish Town marched a pair of godheads, one a few years older than the other.

"Come to Jesus! Come and be saved!"

It was a good area to pick up converts, this, especially in winter. The original inhabitants had been cleared out to make room for a motorway which in fact had not been extended this far. Consequently many of the houses were intact except that their doors had been nailed up and their windows were blocked with corrugated iron and neglect had dug holes in every other roof.

Down-and-outs congregated here now, some of them former residents driven to despair because they had not been re-housed, some simply unemployed, some outright social misfits like meths-drinkers and even a few of the remaining hard-drug addicts. Only four or five sources of illegal supply survived in London, and one of those was a little north of here, a mile or two.

All of a sudden the younger of the godheads gave a stifled cry, and his companion hastened to see what he had found.

Poking out from behind a stub of wall, partly covered by the snow, which was still sifting down although more lightly than an hour before, yet absolutely unmistakable: a pair of human legs.

"What—what shall we do?" the younger godhead whimpered, having to lean on his plastic cross for support. "Should we tell the police?"

The older considered for a moment, and pronounced, "No, I don't think so. Aren't we told to let the dead bury their dead? And the last thing we want is to get mixed up in a police investigation. It would seriously hamper our work."

"I—I suppose you're right," the younger admitted, and added in surprise: "But what are you doing?"

The other had bent over the corpse and after scraping snow away with the end of his cross was fumbling with gloved fingers inside the coat it wore.

"Just checking to see whether he was carrying any—ah—worldly goods," was his answer. "We could make better use of them now than he can . . . No, nothing. No wallet, no bill-fold, just a comb and some keys and—what's this? Oh, only a letter. What a shame. Okay, let's move on. And pray the snow lasts long enough to cover our footprints."

IV

"Lay him down there, nurse," Dr Hector Campbell instructed as he led the way into the white-walled casualty examination room adjacent to his office at the North-West London General Clinic. He had to speak loudly. Not only was it blood-transfusion day—which meant that the pride of the haematological department was in operation, the continuous-throughput plasma centrifuge—but the friend who had brought in this Jewish-looking man with the cut head was keeping up a nonstop flow of excuses.

"I had no shoes on, you see, and there was snow on the road, so by the time I'd gone back for my slippers they'd . . ."

But Hector forgot about him the instant he opened the office door. He froze, muttering an oath.

"Is something wrong?" demanded the girl who was helping the casualty onto the examination couch: "Nurse Diana Rouse" according to the name-badge pinned on her stiff apron.

"Yes! This is wrong!" Furious, Hector advanced into the office. Books had been pulled down from every shelf and lay randomly on the floor, while an attempt had been made to start a fire in a metal wastebin. Griming his fingers with charred paper, he retrieved some of the less completely burned sheets and discovered just what he might have expected: pictures of the genital organs, descriptions of the sexual act.

"Oh, no!" the nurse exclaimed from the doorway. "Who could have done such a dreadful thing?"

"I could make a few guesses," Hector grunted. "What kind of people set themselves up as arbiters of what shall and what shall not appear in print? Now I'll have to send for the police,

I suppose . . . Oh, get on with cleaning up that man's head.
And tell his friend to wait outside!"

On the point of reaching for the phone, he hesitated before
deciding that the intruders were unlikely to have touched it
and hence he would not be spoiling any prints, and during
his hesitation it rang. He snatched it up.

"Dr Campbell? This is Professor Kneller at the Gull-Grant
Research Institute. I believe Maurice Post is a patient of yours,
and we're very anxious to get in touch with him—"

"Professor, I haven't seen Maurice since a week ago!"
Hector broke in. "And I don't have time to talk now. I just
came into my office, and it's been vandalised. Looks like godhead work."

"Oh." A pause. "Well, I won't keep you, then, but if you do
hear anything from Maurice—"

"Yes, of course! Goodbye!"

The magazines provided in the waiting-area for patients and
their friends were approved and donated, according to a rubber stamp on each, by the Campaign Against Moral Pollution,
and hence predictably were dull as ditchwater. Malcolm recalled that at about the same time as he had lost his job there
had been a rash of letters to the press, master-minded no doubt
by Lady Washgrave, saying how horrified parents had been
to find *Playboy* or *Penthouse* when taking their children to see
a doctor.

—The devils. When you think of how *they* pervert kids . . . !

In response to pressure from an influential group of parents
the headmaster of the school at which Malcolm had been a
popular and respected teacher had invited a speaker from the
Campaign to address the morning assembly. The man had declared, with some justification, that the world was going to hell
in a handbasket, and then gone on to claim that the only solution lay in returning to the Good Old Moral Values of the glorious past.

Unable to stand any more, Malcolm had demanded why, if
those values were so marvellous, the people who paid lip-

service to them had involved mankind in two world wars with all their accoutrements from poison gas to atom-bombs. Taking their cue from him, his class had burst out laughing, and the laughter spread, and the visitor was prevented from completing his talk.

Whereupon, the next day, the headlines, bold and black: TEACHER "CORRUPTING CHILDREN", PARENTS CLAIM. And, after the lapse of a week: "ATHEIST TEACHER" SACKED AFTER ROW.

There had been a petition raised by his pupils for his rein-statement, and even now, a year later, some of them occasion-ally called on him. But if they were found out their parents created hell, so the visits were growing fewer.

—And what do those smug clerks at the Employment Ex-change have to say to me through their glass screens? Armour-glass, naturally, because now and then somebody loses his temper at the way they sneer from the security of their Civil Service posts. Why, that I'd make twice as much at a factory bench in Germany! But I don't want that. I want the job I'm trained for, the one I'm good at. Besides, the Germans have started to send their *Gastarbeiter* home to Yugoslavia and Greece and Spain, and some of them are being forced to go.

It had been in the news a few days ago, not prominent.

—Come to think of it, this hospital reminds me of the Em-ployment Exchange. All these people sitting in rows with hope-less looks on their faces . . . But that's wrong. It's a place of healing. It should be a happy place. It should be as splendid as a great cathedral, built of the most magnificent materials and lavish with the master-work of fine artists. Instead, look at it. Barely ten years old, and falling apart already. Thrown up as cheaply as possible, and you can tell just by looking at the staff they don't enjoy working here. Christ, I'm glad I'm only visiting!

He wondered in passing whether anybody had explained to these people waiting that the delay was due to the police being called to the doctor's vandalised office. Probably not.

—I hope I'm not heading for another bout of suicidal depression like yesterday's. If I hadn't run across that guy Morris . . .

He had been to a private school a few miles north of London to be interviewed for a job he had seen advertised, and had known the moment he got there that he was having his time wasted, perhaps deliberately, for the place was plastered with Moral Pollution stickers. On the way home he felt he must have a drink, despite the prohibitive price of liquor, so he had wandered at random into a pub, and . . .

—Fantastic fellow, that Morris. Must have an amazing memory for faces. I mean, to have recognised me from those lousy pictures that appeared in the papers. But it was so reassuring when he asked how I was getting on. The mere fact that someone I'd never met should care about me . . . !

The conversation had taken off like a rocket, and lasted long past the point at which he should have gone home to meet Ruth, with whom he had a date.

—But it was such fun talking to him!

For more than three hours they had chatted away—and gone on drinking, mostly at Morris's expense because as usual Malcolm was broke. They had reviewed the state of the world, the government's incompetence, the hypocrisy of the Moral Polluters, all the subjects Malcolm felt most strongly about . . . plus one other, new to him, which Morris had reverted to several times.

—Can it really be on the cards that we'll see a military coup in Italy, like the Greek one? And that a junta of generals would try to pull them out of the Common Market?

Morris had predicted that, and he'd talked about a certain Marshal Dalessandro whom Malcolm had never heard of, and one way and another he had painted a dreadfully gloomy picture of the immediate future. He had said in so many words, "Like the First and the Second, the Third World War is going to start right here in Europe."

—And I said, "Do you really think there's no hope for us at all?" And he looked at me for a bit, with that odd quizzical expression, and then he produced that little phial of capsules, tiny little yellow things no bigger than rice-grains, and said, "This may be the answer. I hope it is." And I said . . . God, I must have been drunk by then! I said, "If that's the case, I'd like some." And he said, "Okay, here you are. You deserve it more than most people." And like a crazy fool I took it!

In the rush to bring Billy, bleeding rivers, to the clinic (by taxi, and was he going to refund the fare? It had swallowed three pounds from Malcolm's scanty weekly budget), he had had no time to reflect on that capsule and its possible side-effects. But there was that strange point Ruth had raised: how had he known that *four* godheads were crossing the street when deep snow muffled their tread?

Briefly, however, he was distracted from worrying about that. The door of the casualty-examination room was fractionally ajar, and through it drifted a snatch of conversation: Nurse Rouse and Dr Campbell. He listened, hoping to catch some clue as to what had become of Billy.

"Thank goodness they've gone!" From the nurse. "We'll never get through the morning schedule at this rate."

"Don't I know it! Jesus, if only . . . Why, what's wrong?"

Stiffly: "I don't like to hear the Name taken in vain."

"Oh, no. Not you too! Since when have you been on the side of the book-burners, the self-appointed censors, the petty street-corner dictators?"

"You have no proof!"

"Proof? I've proved that a gang of them invaded the wards yesterday evening at what should have been the patients' bed-time and marched around singing and begging. Everybody was furious, but there wasn't anything they dared do. You know how they hit back if you cross them."

"Godheads aren't like that! They're ordinary decent people trying to put some proper standards back into our lives."

"You can say that, after seeing what they did to Mr Cohen?"

"You heard what his friend said—he picked a quarrel deliberately!"

"So what became of the injunction to turn the other cheek?"
—Good question!

In the privacy of his head, Malcolm applauded the doctor's argument.

But, a moment later, Campbell wearily changed the subject. "Speaking of Cohen, what did you do with him?"

"Oh . . . Told him to lie down until we've seen the X rays. But I don't think he's seriously hurt. More shocked than anything."

"Yes, if there's nothing on the plates tell him to go home, not to go to work until tomorrow, come back if he feels at all giddy or unwell. Is his friend still here?"

"I think so. Perhaps if he can wait until the X rays are ready he can see Mr Cohen safely home. I don't think we could possibly spare an ambulance."

Rising fretfully, in need of a toilet, Malcolm heard what he had already heard when Nurse Rouse repeated it, and asked directions to a men's room. She sent him down a long echoing corridor where there was a constant to-ing and fro-ing of staff and patients.

—Poor woman! Shoulders uneven like that . . . Must have broken a collarbone when she was a kid, and it was neglected or badly set. And him, too, the man in the shabby jacket: the way he holds his arms over his belly . . . Ulcer. Yes, an ulcer.

And came close to stopping dead in his tracks as he realised:

—I don't know these people. I never had any training in medicine. So how the hell . . . ? Of course. I've seen the same before, haven't I? Carter-Craig, who had to retire early from the first school I taught at: he used to hold his arms that way when his ulcer was plaguing him. And that boy I was at school with myself, Freddie Grice. His shoulders were uneven and when he grew up he must have come to look pretty much like that woman. Funny I should think of him, though. Must be the first time in—what?—fifteen years.

And, as he discovered he was able to make similar rational guesses about the other patients he passed, waiting for medicine to be issued over a dispensary counter, he was momentarily disturbed.

—Could this have something to do with the VC Morris gave me? I mean, I don't usually think like this, don't usually pay so much attention to everybody I see . . . Still, if the main result of taking VC is to increase your empathy, that can definitely not be bad. The world's terribly short of it. Morris and I were agreeing on that last night.

Then his puzzlement was chased away by something else as he drew level with the main entrance foyer of the building. On arriving with Billy he had spotted a separate casualty entrance, so he had not come in this way. Here now was a fat cheerful woman handing to a nurse seated at a table a little blue chit bearing the symbol of the National Blood Transfusion Service, and saying as she did so, "Haven't done this for years, you know! If I'd realised, I'd have come along sooner. Makes a bit extra for Christmas like, don't it?"

And the girl was exchanging the blue voucher for a five-pound note.

He had known there was a blood-donation session in progress; a sign at the casualty entrance informed would-be donors that they had come to the wrong door. But . . .

Catching sight of him, the seated nurse looked a question.

"Since when have they been paying for blood in this country?" he demanded.

"Oh, it's a new idea," the nurse answered. "Seems not enough people will give blood if they don't. We were having to buy plasma from abroad. So they said to start paying." She pulled a face. "Can't say I fancy the look of some of the people it pulls in, I must admit!"

"Good grief," Malcolm said inadequately. "Ah . . . how much?"

"Oh, five pounds a pint. I mean half-litre."

The idea haunted him all the time he was in the toilet, and finally he gave in.

After all, there was something so horribly appropriate
about it.

"Fry, Malcolm Colin . . . Do you happen to know your
group, Mr Fry? No? You should, you know. Everybody should.
But testing for that will only take a moment . . . Ah, you're O
positive, the commonest group. So that will probably go
straight to the plasma centrifuge. But don't worry, we'll pay
you anyhow! There's always a great demand for plasma over
Christmas: road accidents, kids cutting themselves on knives
they've just been given, drunken housewives getting burned
as they take the turkey out of the oven . . . Sit over there,
please, and wait until the nurse says she's ready."

V

—So what was all that about Maurice Post?

By dint of skimping (he admitted it to himself) on his least urgent patients, Hector Campbell had caught up on the day's list by his regular quitting-time. Being so harried, though, he was already driving out of the clinic's car-park before he recollected the mysterious phone-call from Kneller.

—But he works at Gull-Grant. Why in the world should the director be "anxious to get in touch with him"?

He hesitated. Then, with sudden decision, he turned right instead of left as usual towards his home. Maurice lived on the edge of Hampstead, barely a mile north of here. It would take only ten minutes to go ring his bell and ask if he would like a pre-Christmas drink, and if he were not in little time would have been wasted.

—But it's all very strange!

Though he and Maurice had been at school together, Maurice was the older by three years, so only membership of the school's Science Hobby Club had brought them into regular contact. There had been a lapse of a decade when they completely drifted apart. Coincidentally, however, Maurice's former doctor had retired at the time he moved to Hampstead, and on learning that his new address was in the catchment area of the clinic where Hector worked, he had opted to continue with National Health treatment rather than the private care the government would have preferred someone in his position to choose. Since then, he and Hector had met a dozen times a year, at parties, at the latter's home, or for a spur-of-the-moment drink together.

Hector was not entirely clear about the nature of Maurice's

work at the Gull-Grant Institute. Though he had taken a course
in biochemistry as part of his medical training, he was baffled
by the obscure language of the scientific papers from inter-
nationally respected journals which Maurice now and then
showed him with shy pride. He had, however, gathered that
his old friend was regarded as a leading authority on the structure of complex organic molecules, and had developed valuable new methods of handling viruses *in vitro*.

—And his boss doesn't know where he is? Ridiculous!

They had last met the previous week, when Hector had been
resigned to a dull evening of baby-minding because his wife
was attending a charitable committee-meeting. Maurice had
invited himself over, and they had passed a pleasant couple of
hours chatting. Memory replayed fragments of the conversation, like bad tape full of wow.

"Can there have been a gloomier Christmas than this since
1938? How many people out of work—two million, isn't it? And
this crisis brewing in Italy, and the government making all
these threats about jailing strikers, which I believe a lot more
readily than most of their promises! And all the time inflation
running wild: people walking because they can't afford bus-
fare, the shops full of goods and nobody buying anything even
though it's nearly Christmastime, just wandering around and
staring with those pitiful looks of envy . . . *You've* seen 'em!"

—Pleasant? No, not exactly. We spent too much of the time
commiserating about the mess the world is in. But it was a
splendid bull-session, anyhow.

At which point in his musing he reached an intersection and
slowed to glance left and right despite being on the major
road, for although the snow had stopped this area, unfre-
quented and poverty-stricken, had not been sanded and the
streets were slippery. There, in a narrow cul-de-sac where most
of the houses were empty and the front yards sprouted boastful
signs about impending redevelopment which had never taken
place: a police constable, an ambulance rolling to a halt, and—
a specially bad sign—a group of a dozen kids and a couple of
women clustered together, watching in silence. Plainly they

were very poor. His practised eye noted with dismay the symptoms of osteomalacia, nutritional anasarca, and what, given the fearful price of fruit and vegetables this winter, could all too easily be scurvy.

—Some child hurt playing a dangerous game in one of those vacant houses?

He jumped out of his car, shivering in the bitter wind, and shouted as he approached the policeman, "I'm a doctor! Anything I can do?"

Carrying a blood-red blanket, the ambulance men were heading for a drift of snow piled against a stub of broken wall.

"I'm afraid he's past hope, sir," the constable said.

"A tramp dead of exposure?" Hector hazarded.

The policeman lowered his voice. "More like murder, sir, if you ask me."

"Murder!" Hector echoed, more loudly than he intended, and one of the kids overheard, a snot-nosed brat of about ten.

"Yeah! 'Ad 'is 'ead beat in, just like on the telly!"

And crowed with cynical laughter.

"Get out of it, you lot!" the constable shouted, and continued to Hector, "Though I'm afraid he's right. See for yourself."

He pointed, and for Hector the world came to a grinding halt. He heard himself say faintly, "Maurice!"

"You knew him?" the policeman demanded.

"He's—he was—one of my oldest friends! I was on my way to call on him! Oh, this is terrible!" Hector stooped at the corpse's side, and his last faint hope that he might have been mistaken vanished as he looked more closely at the frost-pale features. Swallowing hard, he said, "His name was Post."

"Yes, I found a letter on him with that name," the policeman began, and broke off as, to the accompaniment of a chorus of jeers from the children, a white car with a flashing blue light on top rounded the corner. "Excuse me, sir. Here comes CID now."

Having performed his rôle as corpse-identifier and relinquished the rest of the grisly task to the experts, Hector stood by feeling numb cold spread up from his soles to match the frozen sensation in his mind. He barely heard what was being said, the consensus that Maurice had been hit very hard with something blunt, that he had probably been killed elsewhere and his body dumped, very likely last night, that it was no use photographing footprints round it because the kids had trampled the snow . . . Yet somehow he could not summon the energy to get back in his car and go home.

And then, unexpectedly, another car roared to a halt and two men emerged, one in his fifties with a grizzled beard, the other plumper and somewhat younger. With a shock, Hector recognised a face he had often seen in scientific magazines Maurice had lent him.

"Professor Kneller!" he shouted.

The bearded man checked. "Who the . . . ?"

"I'm Hector Campbell! Maurice's doctor!" Hurrying over to him.

"Good lord. We spoke on the phone this morning. Well, this is my colleague Arthur Randolph, and . . . You mean it is Maurice that they've found?"

"I'm afraid so."

"Oh, my God." Kneller let his shoulders slump. "Did they find anything on his body?"

"What sort of—?" Hector began, but he was interrupted as the senior police officer at the scene strode to meet them.

"Professor Kneller? I'm Chief Inspector Sawyer. We've had a positive identification from Dr Campbell here, so—"

"Did you find anything on his body?" Kneller snapped.

Sawyer, startled, blinked rapidly several times. "Well, a few odds and ends. My sergeant's made up a list. Sergeant Epton!" Turning.

And the sergeant brought them a printed form with half a dozen lines of neat writing on it, which Kneller scanned hastily. Passing it to Randolph, he shook his head.

"Have you looked in his wallet? It could have been in there," Randolph said.

"There's no mention of a wallet," Kneller grunted.

"That's not surprising, sir," Sawyer put in. "Either this was, as they say, murder in pursuit of theft, or else someone threw his wallet away to make us think it was."

"It is murder? You're sure of that?"

"There's a vanishingly small chance it might have been an accident. I wouldn't bet money on it, though." Sawyer, sharp-featured and lean, looked grim.

"Then I'm afraid you'll have to search this whole area," Kneller said. "Very thoroughly indeed!"

"Looking for what, sir?"

"Probably a container of capsules, little yellow ones the size of a rice-grain."

Hector took a pace forward. "But that sounds like Inspirogene. I prescribed it for Maurice myself. What makes it so special?"

Sawyer glanced at him. "A drug, Doctor?"

"Not the kind you mean," Hector said. "It's for asthma and other allergic complaints. Professor, why in the—?"

Randolph cut him short. "Wilfred, we must search his home. He may have left a note or something."

"Yes, of course. Inspector, we'll have to go there right away. I see his keys were found on him. Bring them along."

Sawyer, clearly disconcerted, answered, "I'm afraid everything from the body will have to go to the forensic people, sir."

"Damn!" Kneller stamped his foot. "Well, if you come to his home with us, can we legally break in?"

"There'd be no need for that," Hector interposed. "His landlady lives downstairs. I'm sure she'll have a key. And she's elderly and almost never goes out."

"Fine! Come along, Inspector—but order a search of this site first."

Obstinately Sawyer said, "You'll have to give me a reason!"

"I can't! Not without wasting time! Simply take my word that . . . Well, for one thing, if these kids got hold of what I'm talking about, there'd be hell to pay."

"Sir!" Diffidently from the young constable. "The body did

look as though someone had searched the pockets. And these kids are a rough lot. Wouldn't put it past 'em to . . ." He ended on a shrug. With a sigh, Sawyer gave ground.

"You come too, Campbell," Randolph said. "You knew him and his habits better than us, I imagine. We're likely to need your advice."

"Oh, Billy! Thanks!" gasped Ruth as she ducked into the hallway of Malcolm's home, followed by a blast of freezing air. Setting down the heavy bag of shopping she carried, obviously her last pre-Christmas purchases, she went on, "Are you okay?"

Touching the bandage around his head, Billy answered with a sour grin. "As well as can be expected. They didn't even have to put stitches in."

"Thank goodness for that! Uh—is Malcolm in?"

"I don't think so. I just knocked on his door and got no answer. I passed out when I came home from the clinic, you see, because of the shot they gave me, I guess, and when I woke up a few minutes ago I came down to say thanks, and . . . Mind out, Ruth."

Descending the stairs carrying luggage, embittered Len Shaw, oldest of Malcolm's lodgers. Pushing by, he said, "Merry Christmas!" In a tone suggestive of afterthought.

"Is Malcolm expecting you?" Billy went on.

"Not exactly. I . . . Well, it may sound silly, but I make a point of not seeing him every day."

"And of not having a key to this house," Billy said acutely. "Too much like permanent, hm?"

She gave him a sharp suspicious glance.

"No, Malcolm hasn't been talking about you to me! But . . . Well, I've seen the change you've brought about in him, and I think it's great. You know what a state he was in when I arrived, a month or so after his wife walked out with the kids because he's unemployed. Even if he was just my landlord, he struck me as a nice guy, and I was worried to see him so miserable. And then you showed up, and ever since . . . Say, can I ask a personal question?"

"I won't promise to answer, but go ahead."

"You're single, right? Well—why the hell?"

Ruth bit her lip. "If you must know," she said after a pause, "by accident. Fatal-type."

"Oh! Like—uh—a car-crash killed your fiancé?"

"No, a train-crash killed my father. And left my mother crippled. It meant I couldn't go to university, and when she did eventually die . . . Well, it seemed too late for children, and that to me is the reason for being married. But I'm doing okay. I have a steady secure job, because of course I had to have one, and I don't think I was cut out to be a wife."

More luggage being carried down the stairs: Reggie Brown, the dreadfully earnest student of archaeology, helping devout Mary with her bags. More insincere cries of "Merry Christmas!" And a renewed blast of cold wind down the hallway.

"Are you going away over Christmas?" Billy asked as the door shut.

"Yes, I'm visiting my brother in Kent. What about you?"

Billy shrugged. "Oh, I'll stay home. I don't have any kinfolk in England, you know, and all my friends are around here. Besides, after what happened this morning I don't feel too much inclined to celebrate a Christian feast."

"It was terrible, wasn't it?" Ruth said. "They were like wild beasts! I really thought for a moment they were going to kill you."

"Wouldn't have been the first time a Jew got killed for being Jewish, would it?" Billy grunted. "I've run across them before, you know. Once we caught one of them planting a gas-bomb —I mean a petrol-bomb—in the section of the bookstore where we keep sex-counselling books and medical texts. And there's a clothing store I pass every morning and evening that closed down after they smashed its windows half a dozen times. They'd found out it was catering to gay people. That made me really hate their guts. Not that I could afford the prices the shop was charging, but even so . . ."

"You mean you—?" Ruth began, looking at him with wide eyes, and broke off. "Oh, I'm sorry. I didn't mean to pry."

Billy spread his hands. "I don't noise it around, but I don't make a secret of it, either. It's the way I am and I feel I'm entitled to live with it."

"Yes. Yes, of course." Ruth hesitated, then turned to pick up her shopping-bag again. "Well, I mainly called in to ask after you, and if Malcolm isn't in—"

From behind the closed door of Malcolm's room came a sudden crash: a plate or saucer smashing.

"But he is in!" Billy exclaimed, and swung around to try the door-handle. Unlocked, the door swung wide.

And there was Malcolm at the breakfast-counter dividing the kitchenette from the rest of the room, very pale and swaying visibly as he tried to kick into a pile the fragments of the plate he had dropped. The light in the room was very low; the radio was playing softly; the TV was on, but not its sound, and everywhere books lay open untidily.

On the breakfast-counter were two bottles of wine: one empty, one newly opened.

"Hi," Malcolm muttered. "Sorry, Ruth. I heard you come in, but I just didn't feel up to . . . Oh, damn! I'm very drunk, I'm afraid. It seems to help."

"I—uh—I wanted to say merry Christmas before I went away," Ruth said, advancing nervously into the room. "And I brought you a sort of extra present . . ."

"Yes, mackerel." Malcolm closed his eyes, looking infinitely weary. "My favourite. Thank you. But you really shouldn't have, not with the price of fish."

"What?" She stopped dead. "How did you know? I told the fishmonger to wrap it tight in plastic so the smell wouldn't—"

"Oh, I just know!" Malcolm snapped. "I know lots of things! Things I thought I'd forgotten years ago, decades ago!" He pointed vaguely at the wine-bottle. "Here, have a drink, help yourselves. Do you know what's happened?"

Billy said uncertainly, "Malcolm, you look sick!"

"*Do you know what's happened?*" With sudden rage. "No, of course not! I'll tell you! I was so depressed when I came back from the clinic I thought I'd call up Cathy and it was

Doug who answered and he said, 'Who's that?' And I said, 'It's Daddy!' And he said—know what he said?" Clinging to the edge of the breakfast-counter, glaring. "He said, 'No, you're not my daddy any more. Mummy said so. We're going to have a new daddy for a Christmas present.' And then she came on the line herself and said I· can't see Doug and Judy over Christmas because this new man of hers is taking them all away somewhere, goodbye!"

"Oh, Malcolm!" Ruth breathed.

"I don't blame you for getting drunk," Billy said.

"It's my own fault, I suppose," Malcolm sighed. "Never marry a good church-going girl, Billy! They can always find moral justifications for anything they feel like doing, no matter how it hurts other people . . . Not that I have to warn you, I guess, on either count."

Billy gave a sad chuckle.

"I was talking about her to this guy Morris I met in the Hampstead Arms," Malcolm went on. "You know, Ruth—the one who gave me that pill." A yawn fought its way past his self-control.

"You took a pill from someone you met at the Hampstead Arms?" Billy echoed incredulously.

Ruth glanced at him. "Yes, he did—the damned fool! Something called VC. Did you ever hear of it?"

"VC?" Billy pondered a second, shook his head. "No, it doesn't mean anything to me. But the Hampstead Arms does. It's just down the road from where the biggest pusher in London lives, and—"

"I feel so sleepy," Malcolm interrupted. "I'm terribly sorry, but I just can't keep my eyes open any longer and I have to go to bed and . . ." Giddily, he tried to walk around the end of the counter, and before he had taken more than four paces he pitched forward into Billy's arms, mouth ajar and uttering peaceful snores.

VI

Maurice's home was in one of a line of small red-brick ter-
raced houses which, when they were built in the late nine-
teenth century, had barely been considered adequate for one
lower-middle-class family. Now they were carved into apart-
ments and even single rooms. Maurice had been lucky and
secured a whole floor to himself when the widow of the former owner found herself unable to make ends meet. There
were a living-room, a bedroom, a study, plus a bathroom and
a tiny kitchen: not lavish accommodation for a world-renowned
expert in organochemistry, and far too cramped for the library
he had accumulated.

There, propped between a salt-cellar and an egg-cup on
the huge brown table that dominated the living-room, was an
envelope addressed to Kneller.

He was about to snatch it up when Sawyer said sharply,
"Just a moment! Dr Randolph, what made you suspect he
might have left a note?"

The same question had been troubling Hector, who stood
by the doorway trying to soothe the landlady; she was half-
hysterical at having her home invaded by police, and kept
muttering about what a respectable district Hampstead had
been before the motorway drew a line of slums across it.

—Right. Since when do murder victims leave notes, like
suicides?

"Guesswork!" Randolph snapped. "Pure guesswork!"

And Kneller chimed in, "You mean you won't let me open
it?"

"Certainly, sir. But . . ." Sawyer selected a clean knife from
a pile of cutlery lying untidy on a side-table; Maurice had

never been a neat housekeeper. "But we don't want to spoil any prints, do we? I mean, if Dr Post himself didn't write that note—"

"It's his writing on the envelope," Kneller insisted. "Isn't it, Campbell?"

Hector nodded. It was spiky and very individual.

"Even so, I'd be obliged if you'd keep your gloves on, and I'll take charge of the envelope." Sawyer spoke with finality. Yielding, Kneller used the knife, and extracted a single close-typed sheet, which he studied with a frown before passing it to Randolph.

There was a period of silence. During it Hector could think only of how cold the room was.

Eventually Randolph said, "Campbell, I gather you saw Maurice last Friday evening, right? That must have been a few hours after we last saw him at the Institute. We were expecting him on Monday as usual and he didn't turn up. Did he seem in any way—well—disturbed?"

"May I?" Sawyer said, holding out his hand for the note. Randolph surrendered it to him.

"Won't mean much to you! Barely means anything to me. But read it by all means. Well, Campbell?"

"Not disturbed," Hector said slowly. "Perhaps . . . agitated? He gave the impression that he had a lot on his mind."

"What did you talk about?" Kneller demanded.

"Oh . . . The state of the world!"

"But did he stress anything in particular?"

Puzzled, Hector cast his mind back. He said after a moment, "I think we spent most of the time wondering whether it would ever be possible for human beings to organise their affairs properly. I recall that he said something . . . Just a moment, let me get this right. Yes! I recall he asked whether, in my view, someone who had it in his power to change human nature ought to do so, on the grounds that while you couldn't tell whether it would be a change for the better it was hard to believe it would be for the worse. He'd been going on about this bee he had in his bonnet about a Third World War breaking out next year."

Kneller whistled between his teeth. "You took him seriously, did you?"

"Well . . ." Hector hesitated. "I'm not sure. We drank rather a lot that evening, you see. But I mention it because it was a point he kept coming back to, several times."

"That settles it," Randolph said with decision. "I'm convinced, Wilfred, even if you're not. Inspector, you'll have to have this place searched properly."

"Looking for Inspirogene capsules?" Hector snapped. He felt confused and adrift, as though he had missed the point of this argument through a momentary lapse of concentration.

"Yes, but not containing Inspirogene any longer," Kneller said, almost shamefaced. "We—uh—we went over Maurice's office today, after lunch. It had been closed up since he left a week ago, of course. And we found two or three little yellow capsules broken at the bottom of a wastebin, as though someone had emptied the contents out and tried to refill them. And . . . Well, that would have been an ideal means of abstracting a few milligrams from the lab."

"A few milligrams of what?" Hector roared, and fractionally out of synch Sawyer echoed him.

"We'll have to tell them," Randolph said to Kneller. "Would you rather leave it to me? But you can't ask the police to work in the dark, you know."

"Oh, go ahead," Kneller muttered.

"Very well." Randolph faced Hector and Sawyer and set his shoulders back. "To the best of our knowledge this is the first that anyone outside the Gull-Grant Institute has heard about the VC project. VC is the—the 'stuff' referred to in Maurice's note."

Reminded of it, Hector mutely sought Sawyer's permission to read it too. The detective ceded it with a shrug, his expression implying that help from any quarter would be welcome, and while Randolph talked on Hector scanned the thirty-odd lines it bore. There were many corrections and x-ings-out, as

though Maurice had been either a very poor typist or under
immense emotional strain. Hector suspected the latter. The
text was almost incomprehensible. He saw a shadow of their
conversation last Friday in references to "the world relapsing
into its old evil ways" and "our missed opportunity to let
people use their known potential", and above all to "that deliberate encouragement of selective inattention which the
guilty among us employ to save themselves from being brought
to book." At one stage Maurice had spoken with uncharacteris-
tic fury about people who, in his opinion, consciously mis-
used their intellectual gifts in order to delude the less intelli-
gent, claiming in particular that while it was natural enough
for men to fight in defence of their homes and families, it was
a wholly artificial process which led them to sacrifice their
lives in defence of leaders who themselves would never risk
exposure on the firing-line because they were too sensible.

—Not exactly news. He did argue it very well, though . . .
These passages, however, were islands of clarity in a muddle of jargon, parasyntaxis, and abominable straining after
pointless puns.

—Poor Maurice! How could he have drifted over the borderline of sanity? He seemed rational enough when I last saw
him. And what could he have done to make somebody kill
him?

Hector composed himself to try and understand what Randolph was saying, but was little the wiser when the explanation was at its end.

"Dr Campbell will know some of this already, but I'll fill
you in on the background, Inspector. Professor Kneller and I
joined the Institute when it was founded eight years ago, and
Dr Post a few months later. Our charter says that we're to
undertake research in biology and organic chemistry without
regard to eventual commercial exploitation. In fact we haven't
managed to live up to that ideal. What looked like more than
adequate funding when Sir Hugh Gull-Grant drafted his will
has been eroded by inflation, and we have sometimes had to

supplement our budget by accepting contracts from outside. But we've always had at least one absolutely pure research project going, and that's the one we started with, an attempt to create a replicating molecule not derived from pre-existent living material."

"But—" Hector began. Randolph glanced at him.

"You were going to say we didn't pioneer that? Quite right. We were beaten to it by Sakulin and his group in Canada. In fact there's now a whole new biology of synthetic replicants, although hardly any practical applications have been found for them so far.

"When Sakulin announced his results, naturally we were terribly disappointed—except for Maurice. In an upside-down way he was almost pleased. Because, you see, we'd been attacking the problem by an entirely different route, and it had led Maurice to something that as far as we know is still unique. The moment he indicated the implications to us, we became quite as excited as we had been miserable an hour ago."

Sawyer's strained face showed he was making a gallant attempt to keep in touch but wasn't convinced he was succeeding.

Randolph rubbed his chin. "To start with, you presumably know that the way we perceive the world is a function of a series of electrochemical interactions. The most dramatic proof lies in the fact that our consciousness can be disturbed even by such a small thing as a blow, more violently by—say—alcohol, and very severely indeed by a high fever or a powerful drug. Yes? Moreover, what we regard as a normal mental state can often be chemically restored, as for example by a tranquilliser."

There were nods: doubtful from Sawyer, urgent from Hector, automatic from the landlady, who still stood ignored in the doorway.

"Moreover, it's known that we do not ordinarily operate at maximum potential. Direct stimulation of the brain with tiny electrodes can bring back memories that are usually inaccessible. That was one of Maurice's starting-points. Another clue came from hallucinogens, which destroy perceptual sets and make things we've seen a thousand times fresh and novel. And he was fascinated by the fact that certain types of heavy-metal poisoning reduce the efficiency of the nervous system and cause significant derangement, yet can be cured by administering a chelating agent, a sort of internal detergent."

Randolph licked his lips. "So he'd been wondering for a long time whether our—our clumsiness in thinking might be due to a remediable cause. You know we are terribly lazy where thinking is concerned. We don't recall, let alone reason with, a fraction of the information we receive. Yet it's in store, and the right stimulus can bring it back.

"Anyway! Among the large number of compounds Maurice had evaluated was one he wanted to study in depth. Only so long as we still stood a chance of being first in the field with a synthetic replicant we had neither time nor resources to divert to it. Privately, however, he'd been doing some amazing theoretical analyses of its properties, and he said flatly that it ought to have an unprecedented effect on the nervous system, including the brain. He claimed it would excite a form of activity usually observed in association with the stimulus of novelty which— Oh, hell. I'm getting tied up in double-talk!"

"In lay terms"—unexpectedly from Kneller—"he said it would amplify intelligence. And damned if he wasn't as near to right as makes no difference. If that bastard, whoever he was, hadn't bashed his head in, he'd have been on the short list for the Nobel as a result."

"That's misleading," Randolph objected. "What we suspect it does is make selective inattention more difficult. Are you familiar with the term? It's the habit of ordering incoming sense-data into arbitrary classes, 'important/unimportant'. I say arbitrary because although most authorities claim this is what keeps us sane, Maurice disagreed, and I now accept that he proved his point. At any rate, in our lab animals the response is uniformly positive."

Kneller nodded. "Yes, rats and hamsters that typically make terribly broad classifications of events will suddenly start to react in ways that can only be accounted for by assuming they're registering differences of the kind we humans pay attention to: colour, texture, time of day, what sort of lab-coat you're wearing . . . Arthur is right, though, to say that's what we *suspect* is happening. We've never administered it to a human subject. But it looks as though it has finally been tested on a man." He pointed with a shaking hand at the note Hector was holding.

"You mean you think Dr Post deliberately dosed himself with it?" Sawyer hazarded. "But surely he'd have told you, done it under controlled conditions!"

"It's all too likely," Kneller sighed. "We had been wondering whether he was overworking—he did seem very tired, very impatient . . . But it's no good speculating now."

"How in heaven's name could you keep this a secret?" Hector burst out. "How long have you been working on it?"

"Since just after Sakulin's first paper appeared. About two years. But Maurice must have identified the original compound a year or more earlier still."

"But you can't have done it all by yourselves! I mean you and Maurice and Dr Randolph!" Hector took a pace forward. "Surely you must employ—well—lab technicians?"

Kneller said in a gravelly tone, "Yes, of course. And postgraduate students, too. But, you see, among the trustees of the Gull-Grant Foundation there's a move to have our Institute dissolved and sell the site for redevelopment. They'd have to go through the courts, but . . . Never mind! The point is that when we realised just what a colossal discovery Maurice had made we called a staff meeting and suggested that—short of being first to achieve a synthetic replicant—this was our best chance of putting the Institute so firmly on the map they wouldn't dare disband our team. Our staff are very loyal, and they agreed without exception. But Maurice had used standard techniques to synthesise VC, so if any hint of its existence had leaked out we'd certainly have been beaten into print. Priority in publication is all, you know, and there are lots of better-funded institutions that could run test-series in a month which our budget compels us to take a year over. So the staff willingly pledged themselves not to breathe a word about VC until Maurice's definitive paper was complete. He was due to present it at the Organochemical Society in March."

"VC . . ." Sawyer said. "What does that stand for?"

"Well," Kneller answered slowly, "we haven't told you quite everything about this stuff. Remember how we chanced on it."

Hector's blood suddenly seemed to turn sluggish as mercury and drain from his head. The world swam around him as he forced out, "You mean it's a replicant?"

"Far and away the most successful ever synthesised," Kneller said. "Streets ahead of the best that Sakulin or anybody else has produced. It's not a virus, not in any standard sense of that term, but it does have this one viral attribute—which, incidentally," he interpolated, "we were no longer looking for by that time! It seems to be an inescapable corollary of the molecular structure . . . and there are enough papers waiting to be written about *that* to keep our staff contentedly quiet, believe me!"

"Right," Randolph agreed. "All being well, every member of our team can look forward to a solid lifetime of genuinely valuable research into this single substance and its close relations. You see, given the proper environment, it multiplies. Living animal tissue is ideal. Which is why we call it 'viral coefficient'."

"You mean it breeds?" Sawyer cried. "You mean it's infectious?"

"Not infectious!" Randolph snapped. "Cold air, sunlight, even dilution in plain water will inactivate it almost at once. But . . . Well, without being infectious, it may possibly be contagious. Which is why we'd better collect some equipment from our labs and get along to the police mortuary right away. We've got to establish whether Maurice—"

"Chief Inspector!" A voice echoing up the stairway.

"Up here!" Sawyer shouted back, and there was a pounding

of footsteps and a moment later the driver of his car appeared, panting.

"Radio message, sir," he said between gasps. "They found a phial of capsules near the body. Looks like it's been trodden on, they said. At any rate all the capsules were broken open."

"Thank goodness for that!" Kneller exclaimed. "So we don't need to worry after all. A minute or two at subzero temperatures like today's, and— Campbell, look out!"

Hector whirled, and was just in time to catch the landlady as she slumped in a dead faint.

VII

As he shrugged out of his greatcoat, heavy with damp, Lance-Corporal Stevens caught a snatch of news being read over a radio playing in the orderly-room.

"—described as 'disastrous' by the manager of one of London's largest department-stores today. In the hope of making up lost business at the last minute many shops will remain open for an extra two hours on Christmas Eve—"

—No skin off my nose, thank goodness. That's my lot until after the holiday. Christ, I'm really looking forward to going home, in spite of all the arguments I'm bound to have with the old man!

He pushed open the orderly-room door and had taken two strides across the floor before he realised there was an officer present: the Church of England chaplain, to be exact, talking to the staff sergeant in charge. Belatedly Stevens threw up a salute, which the chaplain acknowledged with his usual vague smile and wave.

"Just a moment, sir, if you don't mind," the staff sergeant muttered, and went on more loudly, "So there you are, Stevens! Took your time over it today, didn't you?"

"Well, staff, there was an awful lot of traffic—"

"Never mind the excuses! Double on over to the armoury and collect your rifle, and then pack your kit. And be quick about it!"

Stevens stared at him blankly.

"Don't just stand there as though you'd grown roots! Acting Lance you may be, but on the strength it says you're headquarters platoon runner for C company and you're coming to Glasgow with the rest of us. It's nearly five already and we have

to be at RAF Uxbridge at six-thirty. Buses leave in forty minutes, and if you're late I shall personally—"

But Stevens had departed at a run.

"Now where were we, sir?" the staff sergeant continued.
"Oh, yes. Arrangements for notifying next of kin."

"I really think it's *too bad* of Brother Bradshaw to have
kept us hanging about the way he did," fretted Lady Washgrave, seated at her elegant escritoire and poring over the
seemingly endless pile of papers which the last postal delivery
before Christmas had produced. "Having to overprint all our
Crusade leaflets—print those special stickers and add them to
our posters—telephone all the newspapers and amend the wording of our advertisements . . . I do wish he had had the
simple courtesy to give us a little more notice!"

Tarquin Drew, who had actually had to take care of the
tasks she was describing, was discreetly silent.

"Still . . ." Lady Washgrave gathered herself together; she
had never done anything so unladylike as to *pull* herself together since she discovered the quite indecent meaning of
the phrase "to pull a bird". "One must admit it is very encouraging to see how we are appealing to the hearts and minds of
the public who are disillusioned with the fruits of permis-
sivity." She leafed through some of the Christmas presents she
had received on behalf of the Campaign: a thousand pounds
from that nice Mr Filbone who was having such trouble with
strikers at his factory in Scotland, fifty pence from "A Sympathetic Pensioner", with apologies that it was all she could
afford, a sampler sewn by pupils at a convent school, and
others and others far too numerous to take in all at once.

Not that even at this season of good-will the whole of the
post was of that nature. Here was the umpteenth complaint
about a BBC serial based on the life of a jazz musician called
Morton who when a mere teenager had played the piano in
a brothel (disgusting!), and a book whose heroine, so the
sender claimed, was "no better than a tart", and an excerpt

from a so-called marriage manual which recommended prac-
tices so revolting they had almost put her off her lunch.

"Tarquin, kindly bring me a glass of sherry," she said at
last. "I believe I shall need it to help me finish my stint today."

"Of course, milady, right away."

"Oh, it's going to be a wonderful Christmas!" Harry Bott
exclaimed to the children clustered around his knees: three
of the four, the youngest still being a toddler and currently
lying down in his cot. He took another sip from his mug of
Guinness and wiped away the moustache of foam it donated
to him. "Tomorrow we're going to see Uncle Joe in his big
house, and there'll be presents for you all and a lovely tree
with lots of lights on it, and—oh, lots of marvellous things!
Are you looking forward to it?"

"Oh, yes!" chorused the children, who were very fond of
their father because in spite of sometimes being irritable he
was always producing toys and gifts for them which other
kids' parents swore they could not afford.

"And, come to think of it"—he looked at his oldest son
Patrick—"you're being confirmed next Easter, aren't you? So
maybe you ought to come to midnight Mass with us. See what
you're letting yourself in for. What do you think, Vee?"

"What?" Busy pegging out baby-clothes on a line across the
kitchen ceiling, too damp from the spin-drier not to be aired
before re-use.

"Oh, what a fiddle-face! What's wrong with you, woman?
Let's have a smile now and then! Christmas is supposed to be a
happy time!"

For a long moment she stared at him; then she let fall the
blouse she was holding and rushed weeping from the room.

"Oh, well, if that's how she feels . . ." Harry said with a
shrug. "Here, Pat, give me some more Guinness, will you?"

Valentine Crawford stared dully at the screen of the TV,
which was currently showing the Pope addressing a huge
crowd of unemployed in Rome; banners bearing words he

could understand even without speaking Italian bobbed over
the people's heads, demanding LAVORE and GIUSTIZIA! The
sound, of course, was not turned up. The room was crowded,
and a record-player was blasting away, and people were danc-
ing frantically and sometimes getting entangled in the paper
streamers that decorated the ceiling, and in the kitchen next
door the women were busy readying cold fried fish and sweet-
potato pie and rum-and-Coke was flowing by the gallon, and
he was thoroughly miserable in the midst of all the frenetic
artificial gaiety.

"Val!" Suddenly materialising before him, Cissy, looking
gorgeous in her best party-dress—all the more so because it
had been last year's best dress, too, and since then she had
grown in some interesting places. "Don't just sit dere, man,
looking like someone done t'ief yo' savings! Come an' dance
with me!"

—And don't *you* come the island-talk with me. I know as
well as you do you were born right here in England same as
I was . . .

But that wasn't fair. Faking a smile, he nodded and rose
and later, for a while, he was able to join in the game of
make-believe that everybody was sharing, the pretence that
tomorrow everything would really be all right and it would
be possible to walk down the street without buckra bastards
spitting at your feet and buckra busies stopping and searching
you on principle.

Not to mention buckra bitches accusing you of rape.

"Good news for you, Chief," Sergeant Epton said as David
Sawyer entered the office which they shared.

"Such as what?" Sawyer countered sourly. It was not quite
as cold as it had been last week, but the sky was still shedding
intermittent sleet, so that every time the wind did drop back
below freezing-point the streets acquired a fresh glaze of ice,
which was bound to lead to record accident-levels over
Christmas . . .

—Christ, I think I'm going to resign one of these days. What's on my score-card for this month? Mostly, the poor bastards I arrested at that orgy we raided. When I think of the stag-party we held for Inspector Hawker when he was getting married . . . But of course that was just after I joined, and things were different then. Better, maybe. Can the social climate really have turned over this quickly? Yes, I suppose it can. After all, it only took twenty years from Edwardian tea-gowns to flappers' skirts, knee-high, and less than that from the "new look" to the minidress . . . We're bouncing back and forth like table-tennis balls, free and easy one moment, scared of ourselves the next, and having to invoke Divine Law or some other outside principle to help us make our minds up. But I wish I could pick up some real villains! I wish they'd let me! I don't want to be a monitor of private morals! I want to be a thief-taker, I want to see pushers and racketeers behind bars!

—And murderers.

"The Post murder," Epton said. "You can relax over Christmas. It's being looked after at top level, and they don't want us involved any more."

"*What?*"

Epton stared at him in surprise. "Chief, I thought you'd be pleased! I mean, it's the first murder on our patch in nearly a year, isn't it? A black mark on the map!" He pointed at the unsolved-crimes chart; it had sprouted even more coloured pins. "But now it's no longer our pigeon."

—The bastards!

Sawyer clenched his fists. It was one thing to call in the Yard murder squad; that was routine, and done even by provincial police forces, because Scotland Yard boasted the most experienced detectives in the country, whose advice was always welcome. It was something else again to write the local force out of a murder investigation completely, as though they were too incompetent to be involved.

But, aloud, he forced out, "Yes—yes, that does mean we shall have a better chance to enjoy Christmas."

"It's a load off my mind, anyway," Epton grunted.

Sawyer hesitated. Suddenly he said, "Brian, tell me something. Who do you think did more harm in the world—Hitler, or Don Juan?"

"What?"

"You heard me!"

"Of course I did! But . . . Hitler or *who?*"

—Should have known better than to ask such a question of Brian, a pillar of his local Baptist church.

"Never mind." Turning wearily away. "Merry Christmas!"

"Professor Kneller—Dr Randolph?" A smooth-voiced aide appearing at the door of the panelled anteroom where they had been required to wait. "The Home Secretary will see you now. If you would kindly come with me . . . ?"

Randolph was doing his best to preserve a polite demeanour. After twenty minutes' waiting, Kneller had abandoned all pretence Temperamentally he was the more irascible of the two, and now he was into his fifties he felt entitled.

However, he contrived a formal nod of acknowledgement as the Right Honourable Henry Charkall-Phelps, PC, MP, rose and accorded them a frosty greeting, followed by an invitation to sit down on lavishly padded leather chairs facing his broad desk. He was thin, with a pinched face and pursed lips, and his brown hair was receding towards his crown. He wore traditional City clothing, black jacket and pin-striped trousers. His tie too was black. The sole concession to ornament which he allowed himself was a Moral Pollution pin in gold on his left lapel, but even that was half the size of the regular kind.

He was not alone. Apart from the aide who had escorted Kneller and Randolph into the room, two other men were present. One was stout, with a ginger moustache, and even before he was introduced the visitors had recognised him from his pictures on TV and in the papers: Detective Chief Superintendent Owsley, assigned to head the investigation into Maurice Post's death. The other, a man of about thirty-five with his hair cut short and his face almost aggressively clean-shaven, wore an RAF blazer and matching tie, and was identified merely as Dr Gifford, no explanation being given for his presence.

There were more nods.

"Well, gentlemen!" Charkall-Phelps planted his elbows on his desk and set his fingertips together. "While I regret having to call you here on the eve of the Christmas holiday—and would indeed myself far rather be at home with my family!—certain aspects of the case of your late colleague Dr Post's tragic demise, which have been drawn to my attention, leave me no alternative course:" He looked severely at Kneller and Randolph, his manner that of a headmaster before whom two unruly pupils had been brought up for circulating a petition demanding his dismissal.

Kneller snorted. "Such as—?" he countered.

"Such as the fact that apparently you have been experimenting behind locked doors and in secret with a substance of wholly unknown potential!"

"Where better to keep such a substance than behind locked doors? And what's the point of announcing it until we've studied its properties in detail?"

Randolph failed to stifle a chuckle; Kneller had scored a fine debating-point on the first exchange.

Charkall-Phelps was not amused. His narrow lips firmed into a dead straight line for a moment; then he rasped, "But you don't deny that that's what you've been doing! And what is more—what is *far* more—according to your own findings Dr Post was himself infected with this substance!"

"It's quite true that we found traces of VC in his body at the post-mortem," Kneller conceded after a brief hesitation.

"Is it not also true that he abstracted a quantity of the substance from your laboratory?" Charkall-Phelps persisted.

"If you're referring to the capsules found near his body, they were very probably not the source of what we found in his tissues," Kneller snapped. "Our best assumption is that ow-

ing to the volatility of the supportive medium in which we
keep VC—"

"Professor!" Charkall-Phelps broke in. "I am not interested
in your theorising. I am very interested in the safety of the
public at large. It *is* a fact, and please don't waste time by
contradicting me, that both in Dr Post's body and in his pocket
a quantity of VC was taken from your laboratories and released
to the world. There can be no repetition of any such—such
oversight, to use the most tactful term. I might justifiably employ a stronger one. I might, for example, say that never before
have I encountered such a blend of scientific arrogance and
rash incompetence."

Kneller turned perfectly white. "So you brought us here to
pillory us, did you? I might have guessed, knowing how often
at Moral Pollution meetings you've referred to people like us
as blasphemous meddlers!"

"Professor, don't attempt to make this a question of personalities. There's a matter of principle at stake. While it's true
that ordinarily regulations governing research are administered
through the Department of the Environment, they do have the
force of law, and since the Home Office is the ministry the
police come under, when it's a crime as grave as murder which
brings the facts to light it's my plain duty to take action. I did
not call you here to 'pillory' you, but to inform you that you
are required to make your records available to Dr Gifford for
study and evaluation!"

Randolph snapped his fingers. "Gifford! I thought you looked
familiar! Are you S. G. W. Gifford? Porton Down Microbio-
logical Research Centre?"

The man in the blazer inclined his head. "Formerly, yes.
Currently I'm attached to the Home Office, of course."

"But you have no authority to—!" Randolph was on his feet
now.

"Dr Randolph, we have excellent grounds for intervening,"
Charkall-Phelps cut in. "If you would cast your mind back to
a certain contract you undertook for the Ministry of Defence,
which involved techniques for mass-producing a novel type of

antibiotic and which was financed by public funds . . . ? Ah, I see you do recall it. Good. Then the matter is settled. Now, if you'll excuse me, I am *very* busy. Merry Christmas to you both!"

VIII

"Ruth! Ruth, that is you, I know! I recognise your breathing!"

The quiet words roused her from the pile of cushions she had used to improvise a bed. The room was in total darkness, because she had drawn the curtains tight against the cold outside; though the snow of last week had mostly given way to hail and sleet, it was still freezing hard every night.

"Malcolm! You finally woke up!" She snatched a robe around her and by touch located the switch that controlled the nearest light. Shaded to the point where it was not a shock to her eyes, it showed her his face as he rolled over in the bed: pale, unshaven, but visibly less tense than she knew her own to be. "How do you feel?"

"I . . . I feel pretty good. Very relaxed. Very rested. But I'm starving hungry!"

And then in sudden astonishment: "But what the hell are you doing here, anyway?"

Rising, padding towards him barefoot and pausing only to turn on the electric heater, she parried, "That's a good sign, anyhow."

And, one step from his side, her self-control failed, and she fell forward on her knees, clutching at him.

"Malcolm, thank heaven you are all right! I've been so—so terrified!"

"What?" Raising himself on his elbow, he stared at her. "Why? I told you: I feel fine. I feel as though I've slept for days on end . . . Oh, lord." With abrupt fearful realisation, "I have, haven't I? I mean literally!"

Drawing back a fraction, she glanced at the bedside clock

and nodded. "Yes, Malcolm. It's now about five-twenty A.M. on December twenty-seventh."

"I've slept clear through Christmas?" Appalled, he made to throw back the covers and jump from the bed; she caught his shoulders and made him lean back on the pillows again.

"You stay right where you are!" she ordered.

Yielding, seeming weak, he said, "But why aren't you with your brother in Kent? That's where you said you were going!"

"I . . . I decided not to go." Shivering a little, she reached out one arm to turn the heater so that its blast of warmth came at her directly, but with her other hand maintained her grasp of him as though half afraid he might melt into the air.

"I can see that!" he retorted. "But when I flaked out I . . . Have you been looking after me all the time?"

"Billy spelled me. He didn't have anywhere special to go. And if you're worried about the scandal, there's no need. Mary's away, Len's away, Reggie's away . . . We've had the place to ourselves."

"But this is crazy! Did you call the doctor?"

"We decided not to."

"What? If I was lying here right through Christmas and—"

"If we had," she interrupted, "you could very well have found yourself in jail."

He gaped unashamedly. "Ruth, I don't understand!"

"And you better hadn't try until you've woken up properly. I haven't." She yawned and rubbed her eyes. "Wait until I've got the sleep out of me. How about a hot drink? There isn't too much food left—all the shops have been shut, of course—but I have plenty of milk. Hot chocolate?"

"Damn it, stop talking in riddles!" He broke free of her and swung his legs to the floor.

"Only if you get back into bed!" she countered.

"In a minute! I—uh—I *have* to get up!"

"Oh. Oh, sorry. I should have realised. Though, come to think of it, that's another proof we were right." Glancing around, she spotted his bathrobe and handed it to him.

"Proof of what?" he snapped, belting it around him.

"Well, I've had a lot of practice nursing, what with my mother being bed-ridden for so long, and Billy said he'd had to take care of a lot of friends who were on bad trips with acid and mescaline . . . Anyhow, we knew all the right tests, and your pulse was normal and your temperature was normal and you were turning over the way people do when they're asleep, so we were sure you weren't in coma or even in a drunken stupor, which of course was what we first—"

"Stop!" Malcolm ordered, and broke past her and headed for the door. "I don't have time to talk!"

"Chocolate yes or no?" she called after him.

"No! Hot milk and Bovril—I need the protein! I know I have some Bovril left. I can smell it!" And the door slammed.

The toilet flushed, but he did not return at once, and she was just beginning to wonder what had become of him when overhead a door opened and closed and there were footsteps on the stairs and she heard Billy exclaim in amazement, "Malcolm, you woke up! Are you okay now?"

"Yes, I feel fine," Malcolm answered, and preceded Billy back into the room. "I gather," he went on, "that you two think you've kept me out of jail. Would you mind explaining what in hell that's supposed to mean?"

Handing him his hot drink, which he carried over to the bed again so he could sit down in the flow of warm air, Ruth said, "Well, I was going to say: when you passed out we thought you were just drunk, and Billy and I sat talking here for a while and didn't realise how much time was passing, and then all of a sudden there was this reference on the radio news to the Hampstead Arms. The pub where you met Morris, you said."

"You don't have to add footnotes! I remember okay!" Malcolm snapped, and immediately relented. "I'm sorry. But, you see . . ." He thrust his fingers comb-fashion through his tousled hair. "No, how could you see? I'm terribly confused myself. But I can remember everything, and I mean *everything!*"

Billy and Ruth exchanged baffled glances.

"I'm remembering, and remembering, and—and I can't stop! That's why I had to get drunk!" He set aside his mug, his face betraying agony, and she darted to drop on her knees at his side.

"What kind of things?" Billy ventured.

"There's no end to them. Want to know what the weather was like on my second birthday? Windy and raining—I can hear the branches rattling at the window. Want to know the name of the guinea-pigs they kept when I was in infant school? Things that I thought I'd forgotten years ago are coming back, coming back . . ." Retrieving his mug, he clasped both hands around it as though needing its heat to overcome the fit of shivers racking him.

"So what about the Hampstead Arms?" he added after a pause.

"It said on the radio the police were anxious to contact everybody who'd been there the night before, because they're looking for a murderer. And then in the papers on Christmas Eve . . . Ruth, find that copy of the *Guardian* and show him."

She hesitated. "Are you sure we ought to—?"

"That one?" Malcolm shot out his arm and pointed at a paper lying on a table on the far side of the room, almost completely in shadow. "That's Morris, the man I took the pill from! Only— Oh!"

"So we were right," Billy said quietly to Ruth.

"You were but I wasn't," Malcolm said. "I took it for granted Morris was his surname, M-O-R, but it was M-A-U, Maurice Post! And someone killed him!"

"How the hell did you know that?" Billy demanded.

"Why, it says right in the caption who he is!"

"You can read it at that distance, in that light?" Billy said incredulously.

"I— Oh my God." Malcolm sat bolt upright, looking dazedly about him as though he had this moment realised the room was in near-darkness, with only one shaded lamp alight. "But I can read it. It says, 'Dr Maurice Post, the distinguished biochemist'—and that's not right because he told me he was an organochemist, which isn't the same—'who was found dead on a development site in Kentish Town yesterday.' Am I right?"

"Yes," Ruth whispered. "I've read that caption over and over until I know it by heart. Malcolm, something terribly strange has happened to you, hasn't it? The way you could tell there were four godheads crossing the street—the way you smelled the mackerel I brought even though it was tightly wrapped and my shopping was in the hallway—what you said just now about smelling the Bovril, too, because when I found the jar the lid was screwed well down . . ." She shook her head, mystified. "Do you think it's because of the VC?"

"I suppose it must be." Malcolm looked alarmed. "But just a moment; let's take it in order! You didn't call a doctor because people from the pub were being interviewed by the police, and according to Billy it's near to where one of the biggest pushers in London lives. So you realised you would have to tell a doctor about my taking the pill, and—"

Billy interrupted. "For all we knew, it might be a local name for something extremely illegal. I guess it was my—uh—my New York instincts which made me warn Ruth not to call a doctor. Once I did call one to help a friend of mine who had taken an overdose of hash—just hash, nothing worse, but so much that he was getting a hell of a bum trip off it—and the result was I wished a year in jail on the poor guy. I could see you waking up with a cop at your bedside!"

"And especially since I'd have been among the last people to see Post before he died . . ." Malcolm gave a nod. "Yes, it could have been like that. I'm very much obliged. But it was a hell of a risk you were running, wasn't it?"

"Not half the risk you took by swallowing that VC cap!" Billy retorted. "Do you really have no idea what it was?"

Malcolm grinned sheepishly. "No. Absolutely none."

"Why the hell did you *do* it, then?"

"Because I was so depressed I was half-minded to commit suicide!" Malcolm exclaimed. "I wanted to get drunk, or stoned, or *something*, just so that I could forget this miserable world for a few hours."

"Have you been into drugs before at all?"

"Oh, pot was easier to get when I was in college, so I used to smoke now and then. But I never missed it when it sort of faded from the scene. And of course I used amphetamines a few times, to stay up all night studying, but I found they didn't help much. And once I tried acid. But it was a half-and-half trip, if you know what I mean—so delicately balanced between good and bad I never felt tempted to try again. And that's the lot. I mean apart from medical drugs, prescribed for me. Tranquillisers."

Ruth said, "Billy, you know a lot about drugs, don't you? Have you ever heard of anything that could have this sort of effect?"

"This memory thing, you mean? This heightening of the senses? Never. I mean, not except on a very short-term basis. Malcolm, you said you were getting drunk the other evening because of it. Now, apparently, you still have it. Stronger, weaker, about the same?"

"Stronger," Malcolm said positively.

"Does it feel good or bad?"

"Neither. Strange. Different. It was frightening at first, but . . . No, I don't feel afraid of it any more."

"Can you describe what it's like?"

Malcolm pondered, supping at his drink. At length he said, "I can give a sort of analogy. Imagine you took a floodlight for the first time into the attic of a house you've lived in all your life, where you've always imagined there was nothing but useless lumber. And you switch on the lamp, and all of a sudden you realise you're surrounded by priceless heirlooms —Rembrandts and Goyas and heaven knows what else. Well, that's a very faint shadow of how I'm feeling right now."

"By the sound of it you ought to be overjoyed," Ruth said. "You don't look it."

"No. And there's good reason. Because there is lumber up here too, of course." He tapped his temple. "And stupidity.

My God, stupidity with knobs and bells on! How could I ever have been such a fool as to . . . ? Never mind. It's years too late to go back and put *that* right."

"What?" Ruth said.

"I'd rather not tell you," was Malcolm's prompt answer. He was relaxing now, moment by moment, as though within his head some process of review was taking place that was bringing him to terms with himself in the manner a psychiatrist might dream of achieving for his patients.

"Well, whatever it was," Ruth said tartly, "I don't believe it can have been half as foolish as taking this VC pill. Nor can it have caused half as much trouble. Don't you realise I've had to spend Christmas sleeping on that heap of cushions when I should have been at my brother's—that I had to beg off with lies about not being well enough to travel—that my nephews cried when I told them on the phone they weren't going to see me after all?" She glared at him. "Not to mention the agonies I went through when you slept on, and on, and *on!*"

"She's right," Billy said soberly. "We'd just about decided we'd been wrong, and you weren't going to wake up naturally after all, so we'd have to face the consequences of calling a doctor and explain why we didn't do it before. And given my reputation, and yours, and—"

"And what shreds are left of mine!" Ruth cut in.

"Yes. Yes, I see what you mean," Malcolm confessed. "I think you've been wonderful. I'm terribly grateful to you both. And even if it was a fearful gamble it has turned out for the best in the end."

Setting his empty mug on the bedside table, he walked over to pick up the paper with Post's photograph displayed, and shook it around to the front page as he returned to where he had been sitting.

Billy said, "I'm not so sure of that."

"What?" Malcolm countered absently.

"About it turning out for the best, of course! I mean, you've been left with what sound like lasting side-effects, right? You're pretty cheerful right now, but how long is that going to go on?"

"Not very long," Malcolm said, eyes racing down the major news-stories in the paper, then turning it over to follow them on to the back page. "Dalessandro! Yes, Morris mentioned that guy—I mean Maurice Post. I didn't remember hearing about him at the time, but I recall him now. A super-patriot with a fanatical right-wing following, the kind of guy who lays flowers at shrines in memory of Mussolini."

"What do you mean, not very long?" Ruth insisted.

"What I've got . . ." Malcolm licked his lips. "It isn't just being able to remember. It's being able to include what I remember in my calculations. See trends and tendencies I never noticed before. Do you realise I've almost certainly missed the last Christmas?"

"What?"—from both of them, uncomprehendingly.

"When Post told me the conclusions he'd drawn from the news, I didn't really believe him. I just pretended to agree because I was in the right kind of mood not to care if the world did come to an end.

"But now I can fit together in my mind all the hints, all the clues he was referring to, directly or by implication. I can make a pattern of them, the same way he must have done. And do you know what the pattern shows?"

He glanced from one to the other of them, as though challenging them to contradict.

"What the pattern shows is World War Three."

BOOK TWO

Crescent

"I was a Zen Buddhist in the 9th grade, a Hindu in the 10th, I just smoked dope in the 11th grade, then I became a vegetarian, but now I've found the Lord."

—An eighteen-year-old Jesus freak, quoted in *The Last Supplement to the Whole Earth Catalog*

IX

"Look at them! Look!" Half out of his seat although the safety-belt lights were still on, Don Gebhart pointed through the window of the airliner as it taxied towards the terminal at London Airport. He was a rangy man with a prominent Adam's apple, who always dressed in black; skeletal, he did not look in the least like a person who readily grew excited, and in fact was not. But this was an exception.

"Thousands of them!" he went on. "And a cabinet minister right in there with the rest! Even a pop group doesn't get a welcome like this nowadays—and Lady Washgrave has promised they'll line the route into the city, too, clear to your hotel!"

Bobbing under grey sleet like a field of lunatic flowers, streamers hung from dayglo-painted crosses repeated and repeated the slogan: WELCOME BROTHER BRADSHAW!

"I hope they don't catch cold," Bradshaw muttered.

"Oh, Bob, what's wrong with you?" Gebhart demanded. "You should be glad that so many people want you to lead them to the light—you've *got* to be glad!"

"I'll do my best," Bradshaw sighed.

The welcome was indeed fantastic. The hysteria grew and grew while he was posing for the cameras with the Right Honourable Henry Charkall-Phelps, and Lady Washgrave, and a dozen public figures who were patrons of her Campaign, and it reached such a climax as he was being escorted to the limousine awaiting him that the crowd broke the police cordon and mobbed him with crosses and bouquets.

And, in one case, a cut-throat razor.

Just in time, he flung up his arm as he saw the glint of steel, and the bone of his forearm blunted the blade on the way towards its intended target. But there was a sudden wash of brilliant red under the TV lights lining his path, and it turned to grey as all colour and all sensation drained from the world.

"My name is Heather Pogson," the girl who had wielded the razor told reporters. "I am twenty-one. Last time I saw Bob Bradshaw was eight years ago. He took me to a party where everybody was smoking pot, and when I was stoned he screwed me and made me pregnant. But then he claimed it wasn't his fault and ran away back to America. My baby—our baby—had to be aborted. I swore I'd get him, somehow, next time he came in range. I'm only sorry there were too many people in the way for me to slash his face instead of his arm."

Then two policewomen closed in and took her away to jail, whereupon the reporters went to see whether Lady Washgrave had recovered yet. On being splashed with Bradshaw's blood, she had fainted.

It was very cold in the warehouse. David Sawyer struggled not to let his teeth chatter, as though that faint a sound might be heard from the skylight through which they expected the intruders to approach.

Rexwell's had never been robbed. It was a wonder, considering that their products—cassette recorders and miniature transistor radios—were ideal booty for a thief: easy to hide, constantly in demand, relatively expensive, and backed by the reputation of a well-known brand-name. The management had at first pooh-poohed the idea of setting an ambush here, saying how good their plant security must be. But they hadn't run across Harry Bott before, and Sawyer had. When Harry took an interest in premises previously unburgled, it followed that he had spotted something other villains had missed. Using all his powers of persuasion, he had finally put the point over. Even so . . . !

"He'd damned well better show," he muttered to Epton, across the aisle between the stacked crates with his radio to his ear. "Four times I've had that bugger in the dock—four!

And each time he's whistled up the parish priest to say what a good family man he is, how his kids would starve while he was inside . . . Are you *sure* about the sniff?"

"How can I be sure?" Epton answered grumpily. "All I can say is what I've already told you—Stuffy Wilkins has seen him paying far too much attention to this place lately, and if the night watchman can't be relied on, who can?"

"Agreed, agreed. But I wish we could nab that brother-in-law of his instead," Sawyer sighed. He meant Joe Feathers; he and Harry Bott had married sisters. What hard-drug traffic was left in North-West London was notoriously due to him.

"Fat chance!" Epton countered scornfully. "Up there in his big house with his luxury cars and his—"

The radio said softly, "Alpha Hotel, Alpha Hotel, we have a bogey for you. Austin van Kilo Lima Kilo nine-ah-three-ah-six-ah, known to have been stolen!"

"That must be them!" Sawyer whispered thankfully, and they waited out the rest of the time in tense silence.

Then at last there was a scraping at the skylight, and it was heard to creak back on its hinges, and he rose and moved into the aisle directly under it and shone his powerful flashlight upwards and said in a mild voice, "Okay, it's a fair cop, isn't it?"

But Harry was so startled that he lost his footing and tried to grab the skylight to stop himself falling and only half-managed it and came smashing down on top of Sawyer in such a welter of broken glass that both of them had to be rushed to hospital.

—Hope to goodness the kid's okay. Hasn't been much of a Christmas for him . . . "Season of good cheer!" Maybe if you're white and in work and have plenty of money! Though I must admit Cissy's family did their best for both of us. And the other brothers and sisters, too. That's a thing missing from buckra society in London, this give-and-take kind of helpfulness. They do say it used to be found in the old East End, and went with the Blitz. Now even the people who used to be notorious for mutual support, like the Jews, even they seem to have given it up. Trust the goddamn whites not to know when they had a good thing going for them!

Circumspect, but moving quickly because it was another dark and very cold night, with sleet pelting down which had soaked and frozen him to the marrow, Valentine Crawford approached the block of low-rent council flats which was his home, humming Big Bill Broonzy's *Black Brown and White* to keep up his spirits.

—Wish I didn't have to leave the boy alone, but bringing him out with that cough of his in weather like tonight . . . Still, I hope he'll be pleased with these toys.

He'd managed to acquire some very good stuff for Toussaint, and paid next to nothing for it. It came from a street-market. The trader had meant all the items to sell before Christmas, and today had marked them down because he was in a hurry to push his barrow home out of the wet.

Now, up the outside stairs. Here he was always cautious; this time he was especially so, because during the holiday the light at the corner of his landing had been broken by a gang of drunken youths throwing stones, and it hadn't yet been repaired.

—Another ten paces, and . . .

"There he is," a voice muttered, and two dark shapes rushed from deep shadow. He raised his purchases to shield his face, so they went for his belly instead, and a line that burned like ice was drawn across him hip to hip. He fell screaming in a clutter of ill-wrapped parcels and they kicked him a couple of times and ran down to the street laughing with satisfaction. Whoever they were.

—Bloody awful Christmas! Bloody awful weather! Bloody awful people! Bloody army! If I'd known I was letting myself in for this lot I'd never have signed up!

Dennis Stevens had been no farther north before than Birmingham. Now, with the rest of his patrol—five counting the officer in command—he was nervously marching along a road in a slummy district of Glasgow where half the street-lamps had been smashed and every window was dark, though he was convinced people were watching on every side, waiting to do something dreadful.

He'd had vague mental pictures, as a boy, of army life. His father had been conscripted for National Service and spent a year in Cyprus. But those images of a strange country where you couldn't read the writing, let alone speak the language, and swarthy snipers lurked among sun-scorched rocks, didn't seem to correspond at any point with this reality of walking down a cold street carrying a gun.

—I don't get it. I don't get it at all. It must be what they *want* the government to do: send us here. Otherwise why would they be planting bombs and setting buildings on fire and all the rest of it? The more they do of that sort of thing, the more troops are going to be shipped north, and in the end, far as I can see, the whole bloody city is going to be a pile of smoking ruins!

Somebody had celebrated Christmas by blowing up the Town Hall. He'd seen the casualties. Only half a dozen of them, people who'd been walking or driving past, because of course the place was empty over the holiday, but it had turned his stomach to watch them being carried away.

—And who'd want to live in a ruined city?

And then . . .

"Down!" A scream from the lieutenant leading the patrol, and Dennis Stevens reacted just that fraction too late. From a rooftop someone had thrown a chopper-bomb, full of nails and old razor-blades and bits of glass. It landed square at his heels and cut him up, as his sergeant later told reporters, "like a side of butcher's meat."

He heard a rattle of shots, and carried that and pain into oblivion.

"It's a disaster!" moaned Amelia, Lady Washgrave. "The trouble we had to go to, and the expense, issuing all those revised leaflets, and having stickers pasted over our Crusade posters at the last moment—"

"Calm yourself, ma'am," Don Gebhart soothed. "Everything will be okay."

"But the dirt the papers have dug up!" She was literally wringing her hands. "*I* didn't know that last time he was here he was arrested for possessing marijuana! Nobody told *me!* I really think the Home Secretary ought to have known, though, and I'm going to ring up Mr Charkall-Phelps right away and give him a piece of my mind!"

"Ma'am, that was before his conversion," Gebhart insisted. "And isn't it one of the chief reasons for your Crusade that in the bad old days of even eight years ago things like that were being allowed to happen—girls of thirteen being debauched by young men, sometimes even with the consent of their parents?"

Conscious of having scored a point, though sweating slightly because it had been such a near thing, he added, "So don't you worry, ma'am. I've talked with Bob's doctors and they say he's getting on fine, just fine. Like the posters promise, he's going to be there on schedule come January first, and who could ask for better proof of his devotion to the cause of the Lord?"

"Professor Kneller?" the phone said softly.

"Ah . . . Yes! Who is that?"

"Professor, does the term 'VC' mean anything to you?"

"What? Who *is* that speaking?"

"Ah. I thought you might recognise the name. I think we ought to have a quiet talk."

"I said *who is that?*"

"Do you know a pub called the Hampstead Arms? If you would care to meet me . . ."

X

"I wonder why 'Mr X' chose this of all pubs for our rendezvous," Kneller muttered as he braked his car opposite the Hampstead Arms.

"Was it Maurice's regular local, Hector?" Randolph asked from the back seat.

"No, but he liked it better than the one nearest his home. I came here with him two or three times." Climbing out of the car, Hector shivered. Though the snow and sleet had stopped and the sky was clear, the wind was knife-keen.

"All I can say is, I hope we're not on a complete fool's errand," Kneller grunted as he locked the driver's door.

"Or walking into an ambush laid by the killer," Hector suggested.

Kneller stared in horror, then relaxed and gave a snort.

"Hah! I took you seriously for a moment. If that's what you think, why did you agree to come with us?"

Hastening across the road, he pulled open the pub door and stood back to let his companions pass ahead. Hector, going first, stopped so abruptly Randolph bumped into him.

"What's the matter?"

"Sorry! I just recognised someone. The man at the table in the corner." With a jerk of his head Hector indicated a thin man with a skimpy new brown beard, wearing a black anorak, sitting next to an attractive dark-haired woman in a blue coat. Both of them had reacted to the newcomers' arrival . . . but then, so had everybody else in the crowded bar, if only to glance up and see who had let in that blast of freezing air and made the Christmas decorations dance.

"Who is he?" Kneller muttered. "He looks vaguely familiar."

"Name of Fry," Hector answered. "Came to our casualty department the other day with a friend who'd been beaten up by a godhead gang. Funny to find him this far north. I recall he said he lives in Kentish Town."

"Lured by this place's sudden notoriety?" Randolph suggested sourly. "I bet they haven't done this much business for ages . . . Did you say he was beaten up by godheads?"

"Not him. His friend. The same morning my office was vandalised—I mean, the same morning I found it had been."

"Aren't they bastards?" Randolph shuddered. "You've seen the evening papers?" One lay on the seat of a nearby chair which was temporarily vacant; he pointed at it. "Two of them have been charged with setting fire to a Hindu temple in Willesden. Synagogues next, I suppose."

"What do you mean, next?" Kneller countered. "More like already! Ask my Jewish friends about it . . . Well, what's it to be, assuming I can fight my way through and get served?"

"Just a minute," Hector said. "Fry's coming this way."

Pushing towards them with a crooked smile, the brown-bearded man said quietly, "Good evening, Dr Campbell. I didn't expect to meet you here."

"I—ah . . ." Hector hesitated, unwilling to get involved in conversation owing to the reason which had brought them. As though divining his thoughts, Malcolm turned his smile into a grin.

"But I did expect Professor Kneller and Dr Randolph."

There was a dead pause between them, while the rest of the pub chatter continued unabated.

"*You?*" Kneller forced out at last.

"Forgive the cloak-and-dagger approach, but it was a shot in the dark anyway, and even if I suggested this place for our meeting I couldn't be sure you'd take me seriously. I'm glad you did so, though." Lowering his voice, Malcolm added, "You see, Maurice Post not only talked to me in here the night he died, but gave me some VC."

"You mean *you* took it?" Randolph clenched his fists.
"Yes."

"And—?" Kneller demanded.

"And here I am."

"Side-effects?"

"Yes, but . . . Look, get some drinks and join us in the corner. The friend I'm with knows all about it. You can talk freely in front of her."

When, by a combination of pushing and arrogance, they had contrived to group chairs for them all around the table where Malcolm and Ruth were sitting, Kneller took a gulp of his beer and said, "Fry! I thought I recognised you. Weren't you the teacher who got hounded out of his job about a year ago?"

"That's right."

"Of all the incredible coincidences! Maurice mentioned you to me only a couple of weeks back."

"And to me," Hector said. "Last time I saw him he cited your case as an example of what's wrong with our society. He said—let me get this right—he said that among the chief reasons why we can't cope with the consequences of our own ingenuity is that whenever a genuinely open-minded teacher tries to pass that attitude on to his pupils, the entrenched authorities grow frightened and shut his mouth."

"Which is true," Malcolm said with a nod. "He said roughly the same to me, instancing those opponents of Darwin who would rather have lost a limb than abandon Special Creation. But I can see Professor Kneller wants to question me."

"So do I!" Randolph snapped. "If you knew how . . . No, you do the talking. What's VC done to you?"

"Intensified my sensory perceptions to a degree I wouldn't have imagined possible. Beginning with the senses we most neglect. I hope Ruth won't mind my saying"—with a sidelong glance—"that it first showed on the tactile level."

Ruth pulled a face at him, which broke down into a grin.

"Hearing and smell followed concurrently, and sight was affected last. I seem to be able to adjust far faster than before to low light-levels; the rod-cone change-over is almost under voluntary control. As for the senses we don't normally call senses . . . Ruth, that can of fruit-juice I wouldn't drink."

She nodded. "I opened it this morning. It tasted okay to me. But when Malcolm looked at the fine print on the label he found it declared some unpronounceable preservative, and this afternoon we looked it up at the library."

"It's a suspected carcinogen," Malcolm said. "Banned in Spain, Israel, and the States, but apparently not in South Africa, where the juice came from." He made a helpless gesture. "It's supposed to be tasteless. How I knew it was in there, I can't say. I just *knew*."

"Not because he'd seen the label," Ruth supplied. "I'd decanted the contents and thrown the can away."

Kneller and Randolph exchanged stares. "By the sound of it," Kneller said slowly, "Maurice's wildest hopes are being overfulfilled!"

Randolph leaned forward. "How did you come to meet Maurice, Mr Fry?"

"Pure chance. I passed by here and came in for a drink. It was five-forty by the clock over the bar." He pointed, but when the others glanced around all they could see was paper streamers and dangling strips of tinsel. "He asked if I was Malcolm Fry, the ex-teacher, and we started talking. And went on for a good three hours. Making me, I may say, very late for a date with Ruth."

"And he actually gave you some VC?" Hector snapped.

"Yes, in a little yellow capsule."

"Was he drunk?"

"Very. I think I know why. I suspect I also know why he got killed."

Kneller pursed his lips. "Explain!" he commanded.

"Well, the next afternoon I decided to get drunk, too. While I didn't realise it at the time, there was a valid reason. I was feeling the full impact of the VC. It was as though my senses had been whetted to intolerable keenness. I had to damp down the inrush of data, and alcohol did help. In fact a friend of mine who was manic-depressive before he was stabilised on lithium salts once said alcohol was the best emergency prophylactic against his manic phase. Of course, though, assuming that Dr Post had dosed himself with VC, what he should have done was go to bed and sleep the clock around four or five times."

"Did it make you sleep for a long time?" Hector demanded.

"I slept clear through Christmas Day, Boxing Day, over five hours into the morning of the twenty-seventh."

"Evans and Newman!" Hector said with a snap of his fingers.

Kneller looked a question at him. He amplified. "The Evans-Newman theory of sleep states that we don't sleep to recover from fatigue, only in order to dream. The idea is that the brain needs the chance to review the sense-data accumulated during the previous period of wakefulness and use them to update its programming, so to speak. If you go without sleep for too long, you become irritable, your short-term memory breaks down, and eventually you hallucinate."

"Precisely," Malcolm said. "I'm convinced the main reason why I'm here, and tolerably rational, after this fantastic experience, is that Ruth and another friend of ours decided not to have me hospitalised, but leave me to wake up in my own time. But for that . . . !" He gave Ruth's arm an affectionate squeeze.

"When I met Maurice, on the other hand, I imagine he was well past the point at which he should have collapsed into bed. He was already rather aggressive when I insisted at last that I *must* go away, and since he was drunk as well he could all too easily have got involved in a quarrel . . . That is pure guesswork, though. I gather the police are making no progress in the case, and I may be absolutely wrong."

Hector tugged at his beard. "This—this long period of sleep. You think it was purely due to sensory overload?"

"No, another factor is involved."

"Memory!" Kneller exclaimed.

"Precisely. Much, perhaps most, of the overload is not due to present-time input, but to a kind of stock-taking which represents to consciousness all the data already in store." Malcolm gave a wry smile, passing his fingers through his untidy brown hair. "Believe you me, that's exhausting! And not entirely pleasant. But in my case at any rate it has come under control—or at least not got out of control." —

Nodding, Kneller said, "It fits. Oh, yes, it all fits."

"What worries me"—Ruth spoke up with mingled diffidence and defiance—"is this. Malcolm claims he's perfectly all right now, he feels fine. Maybe he is okay. But the only other person we know about who's undergone the experience does seem to have suffered some sort of—well, derangement! Giving a capsule of VC to a complete stranger: can you call that rational? Quite apart from the question of using himself as a guinea-pig!"

Once more Kneller and Randolph exchanged meaningful looks. The latter said, "We're not certain he did dose himself deliberately. You see, the supportive medium we use to—to breed VC, as it were, is volatile, and though we maintain strict precautions it's true that Dr Post opened the sealed vats several times as often as anybody else. Just one faulty filter-mask could have allowed a threshold quantity to be inhaled."

"So you know there is a threshold quantity," Malcolm said.

"Yes, we've demonstrated it with rats, chickens, hamsters . . . It's tiny. Of the order of a few million molecules."

"Proportionately, would it be larger or smaller in the case of a human being?"

Randolph hesitated. "Conceivably, smaller. In view of our more complex nervous systems."

He took a gulp of his half-forgotten beer. "But there's another reason for assuming Maurice inhaled VC by accident, even though he did later—ah—abstract a sample from the lab, a possible sign of derangement one must concede. You see, he was always meticulous about his research work. We've turned over his home, his office, his lab, and found no trace of any record of his experiences. Even if he had decided to experiment on himself without telling us, which I can't accept, it would have been foreign to his character not to leave a detailed day-by-day description of the consequences."

"It's still possible one may be found," Kneller grunted. "Right this minute our Institute is infested with—"

"Wilfred, you're not supposed to talk about that!" Randolph snapped.

"The hell with them. I hate their guts, and in particular I hate that smarmy time-serving boot-licker Gifford! *He* has no right to call himself a scientist!"

"Let me guess," Malcolm said. "You've been invaded by government investigators? Ministry of Defence?"

"Home Office . . . or so they claim. In fact I think you may well be right. At any rate they have all the nastier habits of the trained security man. Currently they're looking for records Maurice might have left at a secret address in our computers, and our work is at a standstill. It's all we can do to keep the test animals fed."

There was a pause. Eventually Malcolm said, "Wasn't there mention in the papers of a note which Dr Post left?"

Kneller nodded. "A weirder farrago of rubbish you never saw. That's why I'm so relieved—I really am—to find you so . . . well, rational!"

"Do you happen to have a copy?" Malcolm murmured.

Slightly sheepish, Kneller felt in his pocket. "As a matter of fact, I did manage to make a photostat. I've spent half Christmas puzzling over it, and I'm no wiser. Here."

Malcolm took the sheet of paper he was offered, glanced at it, and passed it to Ruth. Having read it more slowly, she exclaimed, "Why, it's like something out of *Finnegans Wake!*"

"Right! Professor, Dr Post *did* leave a record of his experience—at any rate, as complete a record as he thought would be necessary, knowing that with total recall he could later compile as detailed an analysis as anyone might wish for. And here it is. Not a farrago of rubbish, but the result of trying to condense scores of different levels of experience—real and vicarious—into the narrowest possible compass. Language isn't designed to carry that kind of load. Not ordinary language, anyhow."

Kneller, frowning, retrieved the paper, and after another reading of it sighed, reaching for his drink.

"On that I'll have to take your word. There's another and I think more important point. If our reasoning is correct, and Maurice inhaled VC accidentally at the outset, the fact stands that he did later steal some from the Institute and hid it in gelatine capsules to make it look like his asthma remedy, and gave some to you. Not altogether, as your friend remarked, a rational pattern of behaviour! So we've invoked the aid of Dr Campbell. As well as being Dr Post's GP, he was a personal friend of his, and he was among the first people, outside the Institute, to learn about VC. Even now not many people know about it. Its existence has been efficiently hushed up. The one reporter who got to Maurice's landlady seized on a garbled reference to it, but the old lady, thank goodness, failed to catch half of what we were saying and misrepeated the remainder! So when you mentioned it on the phone, we—well, we guessed something like this *might* have happened, even though we didn't think it was very likely. And it's a miracle to find that we can talk to, and study, someone in the early stages of—uh—infection, as it were."

"Infection?" Ruth echoed.

Kneller licked his lips. "I can't think what other word to use. VC is a replicant, you know, not a drug."

"I *didn't* know!" Ruth sat sharply forward. "You mean this stuff is actually breeding inside Malcolm's body? You mean it's going to take him over?" Her face twisted with horror.

"No fear of that!" Randolph exclaimed. "We know from our lab tests that there's a stable optimum population for each species we've studied so far. We have no reason to imagine humans will be affected differently. But of course we must give Mr Fry physical as well as psychological examinations. And owing to the situation Professor Kneller mentioned we can't simply take him to our own labs. So we've asked Dr Campbell whether he's willing to"—he betrayed a trace of embarrassment—"well, hide the results for the time being, to be blunt. In the medical records computer at his clinic."

"And I've said yes," Hector put in.

"Why in the world?" Ruth demanded.

"It's hard to explain, but . . . Mr Fry, while you were talking to Dr Post, did he mention his conviction that there is bound to be another world war?"

"Yes, repeatedly."

"The professor and I have been trying to work out why, regardless of Christmas, the government should think it worth assigning a dozen top investigators to ransack our labs, and why they won't allow VC to be mentioned in connection with Dr Post's murder."

"I've been wondering about that," Malcolm said. "They must have ennenyed it, then."

Ruth looked at him blankly.

"N-N-I," he amplified. "What they used to call a D notice. Stands for 'not in the national interest'."

"Correct," Kneller said. "And there's something else. They haven't involved the police, as you might expect in a case of murder. The barely colourable excuse they're offering is that they want to make sure no public funds were misapplied to the VC project when we were working on a Ministry of Defence contract last year. Nothing military. Had to do with extracting antibiotic concentrate from a fungus."

"It follows," Malcolm said softly, "that the government must agree with Dr Post."

Kneller wiped his face. "We think so. And consider what a trump card VC would be if you could safely give it to your entire general staff!"

"It goes deeper," Malcolm said after a moment's thought. "Not just your general staff. But the élite among the handful of survivors. You could literally divide mankind, from birth, into an upper and a lower class."

"Lord, I didn't think of that one!" Kneller whispered, turning pale. "But it would be of a piece with the rest, wouldn't it?"

Randolph shuddered. "Having met Charkall-Phelps, I can just imagine someone like him putting that into practice. Mr Fry, that makes it all the more important for you as our sole human subject—"

"Of course I'll co-operate," Malcolm interrupted. "As to being the sole human subject, though . . . Professor, you mentioned a supportive medium that VC thrives in. Is there only one suitable medium?"

"No, dozens. But the one we use gives the best yield so far attained. Maurice designed it himself, incidentally. Why?"

"Could it survive in human plasma under blood-bank conditions?"

Randolph frowned. "Plasma we never actually tested. It would have been prohibitively expensive. You know it's so scarce the Ministry of Health has been buying from abroad?"

Malcolm gave a wry smile. "Yes, I heard about that."

"In principle, though . . . Hector, what temperature do they store plasma at?"

"About four degrees, I believe."

"In that case I think the answer would be yes. Though I'd have to run a computer simulation to be certain. It probably wouldn't replicate to any significant extent, but it definitely wouldn't be inactivated. *Why?*"

Malcolm drew a deep breath. He looked extremely unhappy.

"I'm about to make Ruth furious with me. Darling, I didn't tell you, but when I was waiting to bring Billy back from the clinic I discovered they're paying blood-donors now, and since the taxi had cost so much—well, guess the rest."

"Oh, no!" Ruth whispered.

"I'm O positive, so they said mine would go straight to the plasma centrifuge. It's a continuous-throughput model you have, isn't it, Dr Campbell? I read about it in the local paper when it was installed. So there's a chance my half-litre may have been so diluted that no recipient could be given a threshold dose. If not . . . well, VC must already be loose in the world. Beyond recall."

XI

"Brother Val!"

Glancing up from the biography of Chaka Zulu which by a miracle he had found in the hospital's library list, Valentine Crawford thought for a moment that it was one of the hospital's many black nurses who had parted the curtains around his bed. The doctor in charge claimed they'd been put there because for no apparent reason he had slept for more than two days and they'd been worried. He suspected the real explanation was that white men in the adjacent beds had complained about the presence of a black.

—Not that I give a damn. I need privacy and the chance to concentrate. The way my mind's working, I'm almost dizzy!

Abruptly he realised the girl peering in was Cissy, and with her—

"Dad!"

—six-year-old Toussaint in person, letting fall a drawing-book that fluttered to the floor like a dying bird as he rushed to greet his father.

"Careful, son!" Valentine cried, fending the boy off with his right arm. A transfusion-tube was taped to the left one, and he had had eighteen stitches in the knife-wound across his belly. The buckra who carved him had obviously not meant him to make such a good recovery. Or any recovery.

Laughing, Cissy captured the kid, sat down, and perched him on her knee. She was looking marvellous today; her coat of bright orange trimmed with white was old, but the brilliant colours suited her to perfection.

"Your mam been looking after him, right?" Valentine said.

"No, me!" Cissy countered in surprise. "They didn't tell you?"

"I thought your mam . . ." Valentine licked his broad lips. "See, I was half-unconscious when they brought me in, but I explained he was there on his own, over and over to make sure they knew what I was saying, and gave your phone-number, and then after the operation I didn't wake up for the longest time, you know?"

"Sure, I heard. Kind of weird! Got us all worried. But the minute I learnt the news I went and got that key you had cut so we could go in and study up in your books, and there he was squalling his head off, and though I got him calmed down in a little he wouldn't come back with me to Mam's, so"— shrugging—"I just kind of moved in. Hope you don't mind." She rumpled the boy's hair. "He's okay now. He's fine."

"I like Cissy, Dad!" Toussaint said. "She gives me nice things." He dug in the pocket of the anorak he was wearing, dark with damp from the snow, which was sifting down beyond the windows, and produced a carton of coloured pencils. "She gave me these, and a drawing-book, and I brought lots of pictures to show you!"

Remembering he'd dropped the book, he scrambled down to retrieve it. Smiling, Valentine laid aside his own reading and prepared to be impressed by his son's masterpieces.

"*Chaka Zulu,*" Cissy read out, leaning to see what Valentine had been passing the time with. "Oh, yeah. I never read about him, but I guess you mentioned him in class."

"Mm-hm," Valentine said absently. "A great man. A genius." He interspersed his words with admiring comments on the polychrome scrawls Toussaint was displaying. "It tells in there how the first time he met explorers from Europe who tried to persuade him the world was round, he made up off the top of his head all the same arguments about it being flat that the Vatican experts had used only a couple of centuries before to put down Giordano Bruno and Galileo. And he didn't even know how to read and write! He must have been brilliant."

Mouth ajar, Cissy shook her head. "Who was this Bruno? And who was—? I guess I didn't catch the other name."

—Shouldn't have expected that to register. After all, she is in my class instead of at a regular school because she got sick of being told only what's proper for a black kid to know. When I was her age, did they tell me about important thinkers like Galileo? Let alone Chaka!

Aloud he said with a sigh, "Remind me to talk about him when I get better. It'll tie in with how the South Africans are making the Bantu as stupid as they want them to be by deporting them to land that's half desert. It's the only way known to reduce intelligence; you deprive kids of protein before they're four years old, the brain doesn't develop right. Before the whites came along, though, the Zulus at any rate were capable of producing a genius like Chaka. Must have scared the shit out of Whitey to run across him!"

And he added to his son, who had turned the last used page of his book, "Hey, that's very good. That's great. Say, do you mind if I draw a picture in your book?"

"Yes please!" Toussaint cried.

"Give me a pencil, then—no, a black one . . . Thanks." Spreading the book out flat, he started to sketch on the next clean sheet.

"I guess they didn't catch the bastard who cut me yet?" he added to Cissy under his breath.

"Shit, no! Don't think they even looked for him. Not seriously."

"Did you tell—*him*—what happened?"

"Sure I did. Remembered what you said: Don't let the buckras get away with anything."

"A bad white man stuck a knife in your tummy!" Toussaint declared.

"Ah . . . Yeah, I'm afraid that's only too true," Valentine muttered. "Well, if the fuzz won't look for him, the brothers and sisters will have to. There he is." He held up the drawing-book. In less than a minute he had produced a portrait of a man with a sharp chin, deep-set eyes, one ear sticking out more than the other, and a broken nose.

"I didn't know you could draw!" Cissy exclaimed.

"Let me see, let me see!" Toussaint demanded, but Valentine held the book out of his reach.

"No more did I." His tone reflected faint surprise. "It's just that I can remember that face clear as my father's. I only caught a glimpse of him, but . . . Well, do you know him?"

"Couldn't mistake him in a million years," Cissy said positively. "Runs a shop near my home. Mam doesn't let me buy things there any more. Mean son-of-a-bitch keeps black people waiting twice as long as anyone else!"

She hesitated. "You're sure he's the one? It's kind of dark on those stairs at your place."

"I couldn't be more certain if I lived to be as old as Methuselah."

"Right!" She tore the sheet out of the book, ignoring Toussaint's objections, folded it, put it in the pocket of her coat. "We'll look after him!"

"You do that small thing," Valentine said grimly. "And make sure he knows why— Hey, son, don't cry! I'll draw another picture specially for you, with lots of pretty colours instead of just black and white!"

"Ah, Stevens!"

Here was Lieutenant Cordery, the smart young officer—younger by six months than Stevens himself, as the latter had learned when sneaking a look at a personnel file he wasn't meant to read—who had been leading the patrol when the chopper-bomb came down. Accompanying him, but hovering in the background, was a civilian in a tweed suit glancing from one to another of the many shields ranked along the wall. This was Rathcanar Military Hospital, on the Scottish border, and every ward was decorated with the arms and colours of regiments whose soldiers had been treated here. Crests and swatches of tartan succeeded one another in dizzying array.

"How are you coming along? All right?" Cordery continued as he perched gingerly on a corner of Stevens' bed. "I see you're still having to be pumped up, ha-ha!"—with a jerk of his thumb at the plasma-flask hung from a bracket beside the bed-head—"but the MO tells me that can be withdrawn this afternoon, so I've come to enlist your co-operation, if you feel up to it. You see . . ."

He felt in the side-pocket of his uniform jacket and produced a wad of news-cuttings. "You see, as the first soldier actually to be—uh—injured in the Glasgow disturbances, you made the papers in rather a big way."

"Thanks, I know," Stevens said in a dull voice.

Momentarily disconcerted, Cordery put the cuttings away. Then, with a shrug, he turned to his civilian companion.

"Mr McPhee, perhaps you'd explain?"

Briskening, the civilian approached with a broad smile. "Lance-Corporal Stevens! Glad to hear how well you're getting on. I'm from Anglo-Caledonian Television, and I've come to organise a segment of our evening magazine programme. I don't expect you've had much chance to watch TV since you came north, of course"—a chuckle—"but you must know the sort of thing. And the point, really, is that now the strikers in Glasgow are turning to terrorism, like their opposite numbers out there in Italy . . . You've heard about the things that are going on in Turin and Milan? Yes? Shocking, isn't it? *Dreadful!* Well, we think, anyhow, that it's high time to provide a proper balance by interviewing someone who's suffered at their hands, and show that we are downright determined to stop the rot in Britain, at least, even if those Eye-ties can't manage it! We only have time to talk to one of you lads, because there's only six minutes for the whole slot, so since—as the lieutenant just said—your name was in the headlines quite a lot as a result of your *most* unfortunate experience, if you feel up to it . . . ?" A wave of one well-manicured hand completed the sentence.

"Yes, sir!" Stevens said. "Never been on the telly. Always fancied the idea!"

"Fine!" McPhee exclaimed. "We'll be here at six twenty-six exactly, then."

At which time, minus thirty seconds or so, a camera trolleyed down the ward in the wake of McPhee speaking in hushed tones to a hand microphone. Having lingered on several beds whose occupants were too badly hurt to offer more response than a thumbs-up sign, the operator turned finally to Stevens.

"And here," McPhee said solemnly, "is Lance-Corporal Dennis Stevens, who was so tragically injured in the line of duty by a vicious so-called chopper-bomb. Corporal, perhaps you'd like to tell our viewers what you think of the unknown criminals who did this to you." Beaming, he leaned close.

"Well, I don't know too much about them, do I?" Stevens said clearly. "Bar one thing, of course."

"What's that?" McPhee prompted.

"They must have more sense and guts than I have. I let myself be driven into the Army, didn't I, when I got sick of hanging around the Labour for a job that wasn't there? And what do I get for signing on? I get my balls cut off, that's what!"

McPhee, in sudden panic, made to withdraw the mike, but he was slow to react and Stevens snatched it from him and shouted, "Don't shut me up—I haven't finished! What's a ruddy chopper-bomb compared to one of these H-bombs they got ready and waiting to fry the lot of us? Think they wouldn't use 'em? I seen the buggers that would, quick as a wink! Soon as I can walk I'm going to quit the Army, and let's see 'em court-martial this phony hero for desertion—won't that be a giggle, hm? Hero be damned! I'm just a poor bugger who couldn't get a proper job! Gang of fucking tearaways, that's all the Army is, only in it you get paid for bashing people about while my mates back home who done the same on a private-enterprise basis got flung in jail 'cause they did it without waiting till they were ordered to! You stupid sheep, you—!"

At which point they finally managed to cut him off.

White and shaking after a violent dressing-down from his colonel, Cordery said to the MO in charge of the ward, "A medical discharge right away, of course. I'm still not certain how much of what he said was actually broadcast, but—"

"But whoever decided to transmit the interview live instead of recording it," the MO snapped, "deserves to be hanged, drawn, and quartered!"

"Yes." Cordery licked his lips. "No doubt a court of inquiry . . . But there is one point."

"What?"

"Was Stevens—well—literal about his injuries?"

"As a matter of fact, he was."

"Oh." Cordery shuddered, and it cost him a visible effort of will not to put his hand to his crotch. "I see. In that case I suppose there's *some* excuse for him."

"There is no excuse," the MO said flatly, "for a soldier to resent being injured in the line of duty. That's what he lets himself in for when he enlists. If Stevens didn't realise, it was his own stupid fault. Now, if you'll excuse me, I'm very busy. After today's confrontation with the strikers, I have twenty-four casualties to attend to."

XII

"Wait outside, please," David Sawyer said to the young constable on duty in the private ward where they were keeping Harry Bott. Not that there was much chance of him running away. A splinter of glass had cut a major artery in his thigh, and he was still on a plasma drip.

Sawyer had got off lighter, but not by much. He had stitches in his scalp and right biceps, and one of his hospital-issue slippers was twice the size of the other to make room for a thick dressing. Apart from residual tenderness, though, he felt fine. He had slept the clock around three times, for no accountable reason, and he'd woken with his mind clear as spring water.

"What do you want?" Harry said, glancing up from the magazine he was reading. "Your oppo Sergeant Epton was in already—isn't one of you jacks enough for today?"

"Yes, I know Brian's been here," Sawyer said, taking the chair the constable had been using and dragging it awkwardly towards the bed. "In fact it's because of something he just told me that I've come calling." He sat down.

"You're wasting your time. Like you said, it was a fair cop. That much I can't argue about, but it stops there." Harry's round face darkened. "I don't know who turned you on to the tickle, but I have my susses, and after I've done my bird I'll sort him out. Better still, have him taken care of while I'm inside. I know how I can set it up without you pinning it on me!"

"You mean by getting Joe Feathers to attend to it?" Sawyer suggested. "No, that won't work. While you're doing your bird, your precious brother-in-law will be porridging too, and if I can swing the deal he'll be in the same stir, and what's more he'll know it was you who put him away."

He curled his lip into a consciously sinister grin and crossed his arms on his chest.

"What *are* you running on about?"

"I'll explain. When you were planning the Rexwell job, you needed someone to carry heavy crates. So you borrowed Chas Verity from Joe—without telling him, I'm sure, because if you had told him you'd have had to cut him in, and Joe isn't the type to be satisfied with a tip, is he? All I need do, then, is let the word loose close enough to Joe for him to hear, before we nick him, that he's sitting out his tenner because you were greedy."

Harry preserved a sullen silence.

"Don't you want to know how I can pin a tenner on Joe—thanks to you?" Sawyer waited until he saw by a fractional twitch of Harry's eyes that the bait had been taken. "I'll tell you. Accessory to murder! And if you don't cough, I'll send *you* up for accessory after instead of a regular B-and-E!"

"What the hell makes you think I could cough about a murder?" There was alarm in Harry's voice. "And anyway, who's dead?"

"His name was Post. Dr Maurice Post."

"You mean that scientist geezer they found in Kentish Town? I read about him in the papers. But that's not on my turf, nor anywhere near it!"

"No more is Rexwell Radio. You were never one to mess on your own doorstep, which is why you've got away from us so often. But it's bang next door to Joe's manor, isn't it? And . . . Well, I saw the body. I can just about picture the man who attacked him. Tall, like about six-four, and heavy, like seventeen or eighteen stone, and rather stupid, so that after he'd done his victim in he'd beat him another couple of times for luck. I can even imagine what Post was hit with. Likely, one of those detachable handles they use for hydraulic jacks, a steel bar about a yard long and an inch thick. Sorry! I mean two centimetres by a metre, don't I? And most of Joe's frighteners are carried on the books at that car-breaker's yard in Finchley. You know that! What weight did Chas wrestle at, Harry? Heavy, wasn't it?"

Harry lay there staring.

"And we all know he's been Joe's right fist since he quit the ring—just the person Joe would tell to sort out a stranger peddling pills on private turf."

"Pills? I don't know anything about pills!"

"Ah, but Joe does, and what's more so does my oppo Sergeant Epton. That's what we were talking about when he came to say hello after his chat with you. You say you read about Post's death. So you know where he was the night before he died! In the Hampstead Arms! There's a bit of history attached to that pub, isn't there? A few years back some of Joe's pushers were getting ruddy blatant in there—and on his front step at that, because he lives only just up the road. Well, that's taken care of, but we keep up our contacts by way of insurance, and someone we believe says he saw one of Joe's boys in there as well as Post the night he died. And to top the lot, he says he saw Post showing off a batch of pills . . . and Joe's man was standing right beside him."

He leaned back. "So I read the situation this way. Joe's boyo phoned in and said something to the effect, here's this amateur moving on to our patch and we can't have that, and the usual car-load of frighteners rolled up and when Post left the pub they—ah—impressed him with the villainy of his trespassing."

"Never took no interest in Joe's business," Harry muttered.

"Try convincing a jury of that. I'll tell you how it'll look to them. We nicked Chas on a job with you. It follows that when he's not working for Joe he's one of yours. We're going to break him because he's stupid. *You* know how thick he is. Far too thick for any court to believe he'd do something as enterprising as beating up a famous scientist unless he was told to. All of which spells accessory after!"

He gave a faint chuckle. "Come on, Harry. As a good Catholic, you've never approved of Joe's dealing. And when a discreet cough could make the difference between the ten you'd pull down this way, and—oh—five at most for breaking and entering, even less if you have the sense to cop good behaviour . . . Well?"

He could almost see the logic of the argument working itself out behind Harry's eyes. But when the other finally spoke, what he said startled him.

"You win, damn you! I knew Chas must have something on his mind, the way he was acting . . . But there's one condition."

"Try me. No promises, but try me."

"It's Vee. My wife." Harry was twisting and untwisting his fingers. "She's got another baby coming. And she's not been feeling too well. If anything happens to her while I'm inside—well, the kids'd be put in care, wouldn't they? I was in care when I was Patrick's age, and that was *hell!*"

Sawyer waited.

"So make sure she gets seen by a doctor. A good one. Of course, I've been telling her she has to put up with it, that's a woman's work in the world, bearing kids and bringing 'em up . . . But if I'm going to be in stir—well, I want you to make sure whatever has to be done gets done to make sure she's around even if I'm not."

"Do you mean that—?" Sawyer began.

"I know what you're going to say! What will Father Grady think if the doctor says she mustn't have the new one? Well, *damn* Father Grady! What use is a mother who's too sick to take care of the kids she already has?"

Curiously touched, Sawyer said, "It's a bargain. You do realise it won't be as easy as it would have been ten years ago? But I'll do my best. That's a promise."

"Are you *sure* it's all right for Brother Bradshaw to speak tonight?" Lady Washgrave asked for the tenth time.

The doctor who had taken charge of the injured evangelist at the London Clinic (of course! No wicked socialised medicine for *him!*) smiled, likewise for the tenth time, and repeated his previous assurance.

"The wound was really far less serious than it appeared, even though he still does have to wear a sling on that arm. Naturally it bled freely, so we gave him a transfusion for safety's sake, but if anything I'm sure he must be fitter now than when he arrived. You know he slept for two whole days? He must have been utterly exhausted!"

His smile was becoming a trifle glassy by now. Seizing his chance to change the subject, he added, "You must be delighted with the way things are going!"

"Oh, yes!" Lady Washgrave agreed. "There's little doubt the tide has turned our way at last."

To launch the New Year's Crusade she had booked the Albert Hall with its seven thousand seats, overruling her timid committee, who feared that hangovers from last night's party-going would prevent people from attending. Despite the chill sleet spattering the streets, the hall was nearly full with ten minutes to go before the starting-time. And some of the vacant places would be occupied by people currently shivering under umbrellas in the hope of glimpsing Brother Bradshaw as he drove up.

Catching sight of Tarquin through the throng of notables awaiting their signal to adjourn to the dais—the Home Secretary, a bishop, actors, writers, singers, the chairman of an international corporation, and lesser lights who by contributing generously had acquired the status of Patrons of the Campaign —she inquired anxiously, "Have there been any disturbances?"

She was always afraid there might be, and when there were she felt physically ill. Her ideal act of Christian witness was Harvest Festival in an old village church on a placid autumn day. Events on this grand a scale ran the risk of counter-demonstrations, not merely from militant atheists and Communists but—more horribly—from Christian extremists, Pentecostalists and Anti-Popery fanatics.

"Nothing to speak of, milady," Tarquin assured her. "The police have the crowd well in hand."

"They'd certainly better improve on their performance at the airport," Lady Washgrave said tartly. "Granted, Mr Charkall-

Phelps apologised personally for that fiasco, but when one thinks of the BBC newscasters raking over all that dirt . . . !" She clenched her fists.

"But it backfired, milady! They wound up making him look like the Prodigal Returned, didn't they? I mean, half the young people here tonight must have sampled drugs, and as for— well, sexual irregularities . . . !" He blushed like a little boy, one of the characteristics which had endeared him to her. "Knowing he's tasted the fleshpots, they're that much more eager to hear why he returned to the fold!"

Before Lady Washgrave could reply, muffled by the walls but still fierce enough to carry to their ears there arose a mighty yell of acclamation.

"Judging by that," Lady Washgrave said, "it sounds as though you're perfectly right, Tarquin dear. Ask the Home Secretary and the bishop to join me in welcoming Brother Bradshaw, please!"

Ten minutes later, to the accompaniment of a roaring hymn led by a choir that had come by bus all the way from Merthyr Tydfil, they assembled on the platform under a huge neon cross and Lady Washgrave gazed out with satisfaction over the ranks of the faithful. Or, perhaps, the would-be faithful. Either way, it was gratifying to see the hall so packed.

—I do hope none of them came here in the hope of further scandalous revelations!

While greeting Brother Bradshaw, she had caught a glimpse of a banner wielded by a servant of Satan, which cried in huge yellow letters SCREW LADY WASHGRAVE, SHE NEEDS IT BADLY . . . but a burly constable had hurled its bearer to the wet flagstones.

So now everything was in the lap of—ah—The Deity.

She tried not to preen at the compliments paid her by Charkall-Phelps, who had generously consented to chair the meeting, nor to feel put out at the far longer time he spent talking about Brother Bradshaw, at the mention of whose name such a storm of applause broke out one expected him to rise and bow; however, he acknowledged the tribute with a mere nod.

"How admirably modest he is!" Tarquin whispered from the row behind where the officials of the Campaign were seated. Strictly, he was not in that category, but she had organised an exception to the rule in view of his devoted services.

Then Charkall-Phelps invited the bishop to offer a prayer of dedication, and relinquished to him the place of honour. Lady Washgrave closed her eyes, preparing to enjoy the prelate's resonant delivery; he was accounted one of the finest public speakers in the Church of England.

After an impressive pause, his baritone voice rang out.

"Lord God of Hosts, behold Your army, mustered against the horde of evil in response to the trumpets of righteousness! We, poor and unworthy servants of Christ—"

"Now that's dishonest for a start!"

Lady Washgrave snapped her eyelids apart. That comment had been made within range of a live microphone, and in an American accent!

—Heaven forbid the stewards should have let some of those terrible extremists sneak in!

But it was no fanatic her gaze encountered. It was Brother Bradshaw! And in the body of the hall practically everyone's eyes had been on him!

The bishop's, naturally, had not. Unused to interruptions, he was blinking in bewilderment.

"Did you call yourself a 'poor servant of Christ'?" Bradshaw said now, very loudly and clearly. "*Poor*, hm? Well, I happen to know you pulled down sixty thousand pounds last year!"

Lady Washgrave felt the world collapse as the bishop gasped and swung around.

"And the 'unworthy' bit, too!" Bradshaw pursued. "I don't believe it—and neither do you! I seldom met anyone smugger or more pompous!"

By now the audience was trembling like a mountain in the penumbra of an earthquake zone. Thoroughly flummoxed, the bishop was hanging on to the rostrum with one hand, to steady himself.

"What's more!" Bradshaw barked. "That bit you started with about the Lord of Hosts! *My* God isn't a man of war! He's the Prince of Peace!"

"Is he drunk or—or crazy?" Tarquin whimpered.

"I don't know!" wailed Lady Washgrave. "But look down there, look at the reporters!" She pointed at the press table; everyone seated at it was grinning broadly.

"Shut up!" someone called from high at the back of the hall.

"No! No!" An answering chorus broke out. "That's Brother Bradshaw! We came to hear Brother Bradshaw!"

"Uh—stewards?" Charkall-Phelps said uncertainly to the microphone before his chair. But the stewards, mostly husky rugger-playing medical students, were glancing helplessly from side to side as the commotion spread.

"Silence!" Regaining his presence of mind, the bishop bent his full episcopal wrath on Bradshaw. "Kindly tell me what you've taken exception to in the prayer I had barely begun to offer!"

"You called us an army!" Bradshaw snapped. "Armies kill! They burn, they pillage, they destroy! They follow orders blindly, to My Lai, to Lidice, countless abominations! You're not an army!" He spun to face the crowd.

"Or if you are, you have nothing to do with the goodness of God! I've been lying in the hospital these past few days—you heard about that? And do you know what I've been thinking about? Do you imagine I've been praying for mercy because I once got stoned and screwed a groupie whose mother didn't have the sense to put her on the pill?"

There was an awful hush. His listeners weren't here expecting such terms to be used in public by the world's most highly paid evangelist.

"No, I've been praying for forgiveness because I've been telling lies!" Bradshaw shouted. "Hypocrisy! *That's* the sin against the Holy Spirit! I've been worse than that smug bugger of a bishop—more like the money-changers in the Temple! To sit back in my plush Hollywood home and tell the poor their plight is a punishment for their sins—that was evil! To bless the tools of war—I've done that, and it was wicked! There isn't a sinner in the hall with more on his conscience than I have, unless it's this bunch of bastards up here on the platform with me!"

By now he had shouldered the bishop aside from the main microphone, and to everyone in the hall it carried the sound as a sudden awful gust of agony broke from his diaphragm.

There were people present who had never heard a grown man sob before.

"Help me!" he forced out. "Oh, Lord, help me! If You ever pitied a man, help me now!"

With a wild swing of his unbandaged arm he swept the microphone to the floor, jumped from the rostrum, and ran pell-mell for an exit. No one was quick enough to intercept him. By the time the stewards had collected their wits, he had vanished.

"Well," Tarquin exclaimed. "At least it's a mercy we didn't get the live television coverage you were hoping for, milady!"

"Oh, shut up, you bloody fool!" snarled Lady Washgrave. "You and your Prodigal Returned . . . !"

XIII

"So who exactly is this helpful friend I'm taking you to see?"
Kneller demanded as he inched his car through the dense traffic of the West End. The New Year's bargain-sales were under
way and the streets were crowded with both vehicles and
pedestrians, but the stores themselves were nearly empty; most
people were simply gazing with awful envy at the window-
displays. It was a grey, cold evening, though not actually snow-
ing or raining at the moment.

"Habib Nasir," Hector said, and checked his watch. "If I'd
known it was going to take so long I wouldn't have asked you
to call on him with me . . . He's not exactly a friend. He married a girl I was in medical school with, called Eileen. And he
works for the Epidemic Early Warning Unit."

"The people who run a computer watch on notifiable diseases, try and catch an outbreak before it spreads?"

"That's them. Except they don't only monitor diseases, they
keep their eye on all aspects of hospital practise, including
drug abuse. They're overworked and understaffed, but they're
always willing to help out a GP like myself, and if people
do start falling asleep for two or three days after receiving a
transfusion it may very well show up on their graphs."

"How did you account for your inquiry?"

"I sort of gave the impression that I'm on to a new variety
of narcolepsy, and want to write a paper about it."

"Neat," Kneller approved. And then, abruptly: "Oh, hell!
Godheads!"

Horrified, Hector hunched close to the windscreen. Half
the street-lamps were out—an economy measure imposed by
the Electricity Generating Board owing to its inability to meet

demand this winter—but the shops, of course, were all brightly lit as part of the government's desperate attempts to counteract the slump by stimulating consumer purchases, so he could clearly see the group of young people, well and warmly clad, working their way along the line of stationary cars in teams of three and demanding alms.

A girl came banging on the window at Hector's side. He scowled and ignored her. Promptly her companions, both burly young men, took station at the car's nose and poised their big plastic crosses hammer-fashion.

"Pay up or they'll smash your headlights!" the girl cried.

Providentially, though, a police-car appeared from the opposite direction, siren howling and light flashing, and drew to a halt only twenty yards ahead. As men in uniform piled out of it, the godheads made off with expressions of disgust.

"Amazing," Kneller said. "I didn't know godheads had any reason to avoid the police."

"You wouldn't think so, would you?" Hector agreed sourly. "Not when quoting the Bible in the dock seems to get you off any charge short of murder. You know the bunch who set fire to that Hindu temple were only given a year's probation?"

"No, I haven't seen the news this evening." Kneller was peering ahead. "What *are* those policemen up to?"

"Oh! Then you haven't heard what Dalessandro's done?"

"No, what?" Absently. Then: "Lord, they're putting a barrier across the road! Diversion signs, too!"

"He's called for everybody who wants a Government of National Unity to stay away from work on Monday. He claims he can shut down the country—factories, offices, railways, docks, the lot."

"Remind me not to be in Italy on Monday, then," Kneller said dryly, and wound down his window as one of the policemen approached. "Constable, what's going on?"

"Bomb-scare in Whitehall, sir. Phone-call from someone who claims he's planting bombs on behalf of those bloody strikers in Glasgow. Probably a hoax, but it's best not to take chances, isn't it?"

He moved on.

"What the hell are they trying to do to us?" Kneller said after a pause.

"Who—the government, or the terrorists?"

"The government!" Kneller snapped. "If they weren't such incompetent idiots, there wouldn't be any terrorists! I mean —well, look at this street right here! Hordes of people who can't afford to buy anything! Two million out of work! Advertisements all over the place saying *buy, buy!* Power-cuts literally every evening! I mean they must have known there was bound to be another cold snap sooner or later, and every winter I can remember when there was more than a week of snow it's been the same—'We weren't prepared to meet the load!'"

Hector nodded. "I know exactly what you mean."

"And because people don't trust them, seeing how incompetent they are, how incapable of providing a decent life for everybody in this, which is one of the richest countries on earth, what do they do? They try and *force* people to behave the way they want! At the point of a gun!"

"I was born in Glasgow," Hector said. "When I heard they were sending the Army in, I felt sick. Literally. You'd think that after Belfast . . . But not a bit of it. They won't stop until Glasgow is a heap of rubble, too."

"I've been to Belfast," Kneller said. "Street after street of ruins. Beggars by the hundred. But the children are the worst. The orphans. Not only ragged, not only half-starved, but insane."

"You don't have to tell me," Hector said sombrely. "Those who could get out, did, and quite a lot of their families have settled in my clinic's catchment area. They bring their kids to me and complain about them screaming in the night—and a lot of them have bruises to show how they tried to shut them up—and expect me to drug them into docility. Undo the effect of years of terror with a single pill! And you're absolutely right about not providing a decent life for the citizens of this rich country. It's bad enough having to fight every inch of the way for adequate medical facilities, having to justify every drug you prescribe to some hidebound bureaucrat, but what I find worst is having to treat people who could be cured in a week if they could afford to eat a balanced diet. You know I've had scurvy cases this winter?"

"Maybe I'm wrong, then," Kneller said. "Maybe they aren't relying exclusively on guns. Maybe they're intending to starve the public into submission."

"Maurice said something like that," Hector muttered. "The last time I saw him. And not only to me, either. To Malcolm Fry as well, apparently."

"And to me," Kneller grunted. "Weeks ago. At the time I thought he was just suffering one of his regular fits of the blues, and I didn't pay too much attention. But the more I think about the missed chances we've had, the more I look at the mess we're in, the more inclined I am to believe even his most extreme charges."

The traffic was moving again, by fits and starts. Without warning, on catching sight of an intersection ahead, he swung to the left and signalled a turn.

"Are you sure—?" Hector began.

"That I'm going the right way? Not to worry! I just realised: if the bomb-scare is in Whitehall, the only alternative routes open for traffic will be streets we'd pass along if we continued straight ahead. If I go this way, we can cut across them at junctions where there are traffic-lights. We ought to save— hmm!—about eighteen or nineteen minutes."

"You must know London as well as a taxi-driver," Hector said. "I have no sense of direction to speak of."

Kneller looked briefly surprised. "Nor do I, really! But . . . well, this just seems like an obvious idea. I hope I'm right. Ah—you were talking about Malcolm a moment ago. I presume he was still all right when you saw him today?"

"Oh, he's perfectly fit. No doubt of it. I did something new this morning, though, which I was going to tell you about. Remember I sent to MENSA for one of their Cattell Three tests and gave it to him the other day?"

"Yes, you told me."

"Well, he didn't score any higher on that than you'd have expected—he says he was rated 135 when he was at school, about what you might guess, I think, and MENSA scored his paper at 139, which is too close to be significant. But—well, do you know the Christmas general-knowledge test they always reprint in the *Guardian*?"

"The one from King William School that's supposed to occupy the boys for the whole of their four-week holiday?"

"That's right. The answers won't be published for at least another fortnight. So I gave it to him. He does read the *Guardian* himself, but he swears he hasn't researched the quiz because he's been far too busy. I believe him."

Hector licked his lips. "Well, he answered ninety-seven of the questions. The other three he left blank. Said he didn't know and wouldn't pretend."

"And—?"

"And during my lunch-break I made a random check of a dozen of his answers. Phoned a librarian I know. All correct, according to the *Encylopaedia Britannica*."

"So he's probably telling the truth about what VC has done to his memory."

"Yes. I don't think there's any doubt about it. Those question-papers are deliberately made so hard that nobody without eidetic recall can cope—and at that you'd have to be extremely widely read. I think we can take it for granted that Malcolm Fry does now have total recall."

"And seems physically fit," Kneller muttered. "Well, if there are no untoward side-effects . . . You were going to try and talk to his girl-friend, and this lodger who helped to nurse him over Christmas."

"I've seen them both, yes. Billy Cohen isn't much help—he only met Malcolm five months ago when he answered an advertisement for a room to let and Malcolm doesn't socialise very much with his lodgers. Small wonder, because apart from Billy they sound like a terribly dreary bunch. And frankly Ruth can't tell me much more than Billy, because she met him even more recently, at a party about three months ago. She has given a couple of important hints, though."

"Such as?"

"Well, she let it fall that he's become a spectacularly good lover, almost overnight. In fact she's decided to move in with him and disregard the scandal and the complaints of the neighbours. She says she can't imagine ever meeting another man who would turn her on so well."

Braking for yet another stop-light—but they were making good progress on the roundabout route he had switched to—Kneller said, "That sounds like a real boon! Lord, when I was in my mid-thirties, I thought the millennium had arrived, you know. I had . . . Well, I had a rather repressed upbringing. It wasn't that my parents wanted me to be inhibited; rather, it was that to find out how to make me uninhibited they had to go and look up a book! Twenty years ago, fifteen, I was really getting excited about the relaxed and casual attitudes of my students. I thought maybe we were going to digest this conflict between the Christian injunction to get married and stay married, and the simple fact that nowadays we live so much longer it's a miracle if you can settle for a single partner, so— Sorry! It's a hobbyhorse of mine, that. I didn't mean to go off at a tangent."

"The only other point I was going to make," Hector said, "was that apparently Malcolm has had a couple of bouts of extreme depression. But this may well have no connection with VC. Wouldn't you expect someone to be depressed in his position? You know his wife packed the kids in the car because he'd been six months out of work, and drove off, and now she's found someone else and wants to prevent him seeing his own children ever again? With or without VC, that plus the state of the world could easily explain his depression."

"Agreed," Kneller said with a grimace.

"So on balance I'm very optimistic about VC," Hector concluded.

"I'd like to be. I have reservations, though. There are people I've run across in the Civil Service, the armed forces, commerce, even the academic world, who would cheerfully exploit the stuff for the purpose we mentioned the other evening: creating an élite and a subcaste. I'm not joking, you know . . . Well, here's the right road—and by a miracle there's a parking-space right outside the place we're going to!"

Hector said in surprise, "But that's where Habib always parks!"

"Damn! Is it? I hope he hasn't got sick of waiting!"

The door of the apartment opened cautiously on a security-chain and a tremulous voice said, "What do you want?"

"Eileen! It's me—Hector!"

"Oh, thank goodness! Come in!" Eileen, a pretty blonde looking very tired and miserable, released the chain. "I'm sorry, Habib isn't here. I gather he found exactly what you wanted, and he's left you a note. But he had to go out when they told us about the bombing."

"You mean it actually went off?" Hector demanded. "No wonder we were diverted! That's why we're late."

Locking the door again, Eileen stared at him. "But Regent's Park is nowhere near your route, surely!"

"I think we must be talking about two different bombs," Hector said slowly. "Why Regent's Park?"

"Because they blew up the Islamic Cultural Centre, that's why! Habib isn't exactly devout, but when something like this happens . . . They think it was godhead work. At any rate there were bloody great crosses painted all over everywhere."

She hesitated. "Look, forgive me, but I'm just going to hand over the note Habib left and turn you out again. I can't stand company tonight. I want to sit by myself and—and cry my eyes out! It's terrifying! The world feels as though we're on a roller-coaster ride to Armageddon!"

Back in the car Kneller said, "That about sums up my own view."

"And mine," Hector said, examining the sheet of paper—a

computer print-out—which Eileen had given him. "Hmm! How interesting! I recognise one of these names."

"Which one? And how many are there?"

"Five. I can't place Bott or Bradshaw or Crawford or Jarman-Sawyer, but 'Dennis Horace Stevens' sounds like the first soldier to get hurt in the Glasgow riots—the one who caused a scandal when he appeared on TV and told the world what he thinks of the army."

"I'm not with you," Kneller said after a pause.

"Likely not. I didn't see it in the London papers. But my sister was watching, and wrote to me about it. To top it off he's vanished from Rathcanar Hospital. Walked out with heaven knows how many stitches in him. I wonder how the poor devil's feeling—if he's alive!"

Kneller took and scanned the list. "I think I recognise another of these names," he said.

"Which of them?"

"Didn't you know that Brother Bradshaw is the same as Bob Bradshaw, who used to star in the TV series *Gunslinger?*"

"Of course, but . . . Oh! 'Bradshaw Robert Emmanuel'?"

"It would account for his extraordinary behaviour at the Albert Hall, wouldn't it?" Kneller restarted the car. "I suggest we call on Malcolm and find out what he thinks."

"Professor, you must concur with Maurice," Hector said.

"How do you mean?"

"In his view, Malcolm was a deserving case likely to benefit from VC. Are you convinced he was right?"

Kneller looked faintly surprised. "Well, on present evidence—"

Hector cut in. "Apparently you've stopped worrying about VC, as Maurice did! Last time I talked to Randolph, he appeared to be tending the same way. I can't help wondering . . . Well, you do work in the same labs, and even if you don't open the culture-vats as often as Maurice used to . . ."

Kneller had turned paper-pale. He said after a dreadful moment of silence, "Yes, I see. Tomorrow I'll try and dodge Gifford long enough to run the necessary tests."

XIV

"I don't get it!" complained Sergeant Epton.

"Get what?" Dàvid Sawyer countered. Officially he was still on sick-leave; however, for what reason he could not guess, since he woke up in hospital his mind had been haunted by a nonstop sequence of surprising insights. His brain was whirling like a Catherine wheel, throwing off sparks of brilliance, and today he had been unable to endure the tension any longer, so he had come to the station to pass on some of his ideas, and Epton was overwhelmed.

"You know very well what I mean, Chief. Chas Verity coughed in under the hour when we taxed him with the Post murder, and that was your suggestion. Soon as I had the statement signed, I called the murder squad, and were they delighted? Not a bit of it—they acted as though they'd been done an injury! On top of which, thanks to you we finally nailed Joe Feathers, caught him red-handed. Wouldn't you expect a commendation, at least? Instead—*well!*"

"Not really," Sawyer sighed.

"And now this lot!" Epton went on. He tapped the sheet on which he had noted down what Sawyer had been talking about this past half-hour. "If even a couple of these work out, we could see off some of the nastiest villains on the patch— What? Did you say you weren't expecting a commendation?"

Sawyer rose and limped to the window overlooking the yard. He said, his back turned, "Frankly, no. No more than I was expecting jail for the bastard who drove that car into the Italian demonstration before Christmas. You remember he broke a man's legs? And he got away with it!"

"As good as," Epton admitted. "What's a twenty-pound fine these days?"

"What you get for parking in the wrong place!" Sawyer sighed. "Well, it's all of a piece, you know."

"What with?"

"With them not being happy at having the Post case cleared up on the local level. Who gave orders for it to be taken out of our hands? The Home Secretary himself! And who did he give it to? Owsley! Owsley isn't a jack like you and me—he's been with Special Branch most of the time since he joined. Murder isn't his line. What he's good at is waking anarchists at three in the morning and turning their rooms over!" He gave a harsh laugh. "No wonder Charkall-Phelps likes him so much!"

"You've become very bitter all of a sudden, Chief," Epton said after a pause.

"I suppose I have. But there are reasons. I've been thinking over my sins of omission. I have left undone those things that I ought to have done."

"I didn't know you were a churchgoer," Epton ventured.

"I'm not. I've been turned off it. But the phrases tend to stick, don't they?" Sawyer swung back to face the sergeant. "By the way, you had Harry Bott in court this morning, didn't you? What happened—remanded in custody?"

"What else?" Epton grinned. "That ought to make you feel pleased with yourself, if nothing else can. As a matter of fact . . ."

"Yes?"

"He asked to see you. I said you were still on sick-leave, naturally. But he was very persistent."

"Then fix me an interview!" Sawyer said. "I'd rather Harry than some people I could name. An honest villain is a cut above one who smiles and smiles."

"What? Oh! Is that . . . Shakespeare?"

"Right in one. *Hamlet*."

"Been reading it up in hospital, have you?"

"No, thinking about it. Thinking about a lot of things. I told you. For some reason I simply can't stop."

"Hello, Harry," he said, half an hour later.

"Hello," grunted Harry Bott from the other side of the plain wooden table which, with three equally plain chairs, furnished the remand centre's interview room.

"So what do you want to see me about?" Sawyer went on, sitting down. "If it's Vera, I—uh—I tracked down the right kind of doctor for her."

"I heard. Thanks." Harry put his fingertips together, closed his eyes, seemed to squeeze himself; his jaw-muscles knotted and his elbows pressed into his ribs. He said after a pause, eyes still shut, "Mr Sawyer, I got to talk to somebody. I'm scared of going out of my mind."

Sawyer was startled, but kept his tone carefully neutral. "In what way?"

"I—I can't face going back to jail! You know I done a bit of porridge before, don't you? I was still pretty much a kid— twenty-two—and it was only six months, four after good behaviour, but I remember clear as crystal what it was like, and . . . Oh, sweet suffering Mary mother of God! Being shut up with two other men in a cell for years on end—I'd go crazy! My mind is spinning and spinning and all the time I keep remembering *and it won't stop!*"

There was a dead pause. Harry took advantage of it to collect himself, while Sawyer simply stared at him.

—But that's exactly how *I* feel! I don't know what the hell's happened to me, let alone to him, so— Oh, no. I don't see how, but . . . Dr Randolph. What he said about VC.

It was clear in his mind in the space of a heartbeat and all his earlier facile assumptions blew away on the wind.

—What do we have in common? Same hospital, same time . . . I'm going to start digging into this! Contact Kneller!

"So?" was all he said aloud, however.

"So I want to make a deal, Mr Sawyer."

"Try me. I'm listening."

Harry licked his lips. "Just what I'd have expected you to say, Mr Sawyer. I've always thought of you as a square jack, not like some of the bent bastards I've bumped into. I know you'd rather knock off real villains than people like me . . . Funny thing for me to say, isn't it? But at least I've bothered big companies, chain-stores, the sort of tickle where people get hit in the pocket, not the guts! Except once. For about a year. I was a—a frightener. Did you know?"

"And . . . ?"

"And I got sick of it. We used dogs, we used petrol-bombs, we shipped in tarts and junkies, just to force people out of their homes so a bastard with more cash than he knew what to do with already could tear down houses and put up luxury flats. I could finger that bugger for you. Didn't think I could, but I've been working it out in my mind. Little hints, little clues . . . And how would you like someone who owes half a million in tax? How'd you like a crook solicitor who takes a thousand nicker a go to supply perjured witnesses? How'd you like—?"

Sawyer held up his hand. "Very much. And you know it! But what do I have to do to get it?"

"Spring me and get me out of the country. To Australia. With Vee and the kids."

Sawyer whistled.

"I know it's a lot to ask!" Harry pleaded. "But—but I've got to go straight now, Mr Sawyer. Just *got* to! I simply couldn't carry on like I used! There was anguish in his voice. He literally wrung his hands. "Thinking back on my spell as a frightener, I can't sleep! I swear it! What I did to people who'd never harmed me or anyone . . . !"

"You know something funny?" Sawyer said. "I believe you. There's a million who wouldn't. But I do."

"Are ye no' feeling well?" inquired the plump old body behind the counter of the little sub-post office, peering at Dennis Stevens over her glasses.

"Och, I'm fine," he muttered in reply, planting the parcel he had brought on the scales beside her. He gave an anxious glance around. This place was far enough away from the centre of the Glasgow disturbances for there not yet to be an armed soldier on guard at the door in case of a raid by strikers after money to supplement their union's strike fund. Three days ago they had audaciously carried out one in broad daylight which netted almost four thousand pounds.

—And bloody good luck to them, I say!

But he hoped to heaven the postmistress wasn't going to try and engage him in a long conversation. He was getting the hang of the local accent well enough to make a sentence or two pass muster, but it was terribly difficult to concentrate. What he had just told her was a lie.

He hurt.

Well, he had been expecting that. But he had carefully duplicated the treatment they'd been giving him at the hospital—he could remember, as clearly as though they were still before him, the labels on the packets of dressings and the phials of antibiotic which the MO had used, and the gradation to which the hypodermics had been filled, and the intervals between injections, and he had raided one of the largest chemist's shops in the city, eluding locks and burglar-alarms with ease, and possessed himself of all the necessary equipment and drugs.

And other things as well, which were here in the parcel.

But something, nonetheless, wasn't right. There was a wetness between his legs, and this morning when he awoke there had been a yellow ooze from the hideous, hateful, horrible wound the stitches closed. He felt giddy, and now and then his eyes drifted out of focus despite his best efforts. Ideas came and went in his mind—went before he had time to examine them properly. It was going to be necessary after all to appeal to a doctor. But how? Would the strikers, embattled in their no-go zone, where soldiers dared not venture on foot, welcome him if he admitted who he was? Surely they would—surely they must! Because anyone else would doubtless call the police immediately and have him arrested . . .

"What?" he said foggily, realising that the plump woman had asked a question.

"I said first class, or second?" the woman repeated. And went on, staring at him: "Are ye *sure* ye're no' ill?"

"I have a heidache!" he answered curtly. "Mak' it first! The sooner it arrives, the be'er!"

He glanced one final time at the address, confirming he had remembered it correctly: *Mrs June Cordery, No. 35, Officers' Married Quarters* . . . Yes, no errors in that. He felt in his pocket for coins to pay the postage. Under his fingertips, squelching foulness.

—Oh, no! It's getting worse by the minute! But what's happened to me is nothing compared to what will happen to that bastard's wife when she opens what looks so much like a present from her husband, what with its Glasgow postmark and everything. I hope she's leaning close when it blows up. I hope it blinds her—no, only in one eye, because I want her to see the look of loathing on her husband's face next time they meet . . .

The world swam. The day turned dark all of a sudden. The floor rocked and abruptly rose to hit him on the side. At a very great distance he heard a cry of alarm.

—But I haven't paid for the parcel yet. I must. I . . .

Only it seemed like too much of an effort to say so.

"I shouldn't have brought you this way round," Cissy muttered as she felt Valentine leaning on her instead of merely holding her arm companionably. It was dark and cold here on the narrow street; as in most low-income areas of London— and othe British cities—they had switched off not half the street-lamps, but three out of four of them. Who, after all, gave a damn about people who had to live in slummy districts like this one?

"Keep going!" Valentine directed, gritting his teeth. "I ought to see what the brothers and sisters did to the bastard who carved me!"

Cissy gave him a doubtful glance. Somehow, in a way she could not fathom, that last remark had rung hollow.

—Forced? Yes. But . . . Oh, well: here we are.

And they rounded a corner, waving hello to a newspaper-seller who (exceptionally, in London) was black, and stood shivering as he presided over poster-displays announcing GLASGOW DESERTER CAPTURED and ITALIAN GOVERNMENT DEFEATED, and came in sight of what had been a grocery store.

Now, its entire frontage was boarded up and there was a for-sale sign straining in the wind, threatening to pull loose the nails that secured it to a black-painted pole, and smears of smoke-grey washed up the wall towards the windows of the small apartment above it.

"There!" Cissy said with pride. "And when he came rushing out we grabbed him and tore his pants off and left him right here in the street to watch the place burn!"

Valentine said nothing, staring at the ruined shop.

"Val?" She drew back a fraction, turning to him. "Is—?"

"Is something wrong?" he interrupted roughly. "Yes, *something!* I don't know what!"

"Don't tell me they turned you out of hospital too soon!" Leaping to an obvious conclusion. "I did think it was kind of—"

"No, not that." He bit his lip. "My body's mending okay, no doubt of it. Think I'd have let them buckra doctors turn me out before I was well on the way to being healed? No, what's wrong is . . ."

He hesitated. "I don't get it. It goes into words, and then it doesn't make sense."

"Explain!" Cissy ordered, hunching the fur collar of her coat higher around her pretty face.

"It's so complicated . . . To start with, though: the way you've helped me and Toussaint. I—uh—I love you for it."

"Man, I've loved you since the day I met you!" Cissy threw

her arms around him and administered a smacking kiss on his cold dark cheek. "So what else is new?"

"So it makes me feel bad to know that because I got cut up you got involved in—that."

"It was a pleasure! How often do you watch one of them bastards swallowing his own medicine?"

"It's not like that. It's— Ah, *shit!* Let's get on home. But I hope one thing. Really do."

"What?"

"You never have to do that again." With a jerk of his thumb at the shop as he moved away, stiffly to favour his half-knit belly-muscles.

"So long as they walk on us like we were dirt, we'll have to keep it up!" Cissy snapped.

"Yeah, but . . . Cis honey, I got things cooking in this head of mine. I'll tell you about them when we get back. Right now, you go in the baker's, and find some cake for Toussaint's tea."

XV

Tonight snow in big soft pillow-down flakes was adding the latest of many layers to the winter-glaze of London's streets. Snow, thaw, frost, sleet, frost, snow . . . It had been going on since November. Caught by surprise as usual, the city council had snowploughs enough only for a few crucial thoroughfares. Elsewhere they had fallen back on men with shovels and truckloads of sand, and in minor streets not even that much effort was being made any longer. Like miniaturised geological strata, ice and sand in alternation had compacted to the level of the kerbstones or higher, embedding rubbish for fossils. No council employees had been spared to clear litter-bins since early December, and all of them had been overflowing for weeks.

Now, at the end of this narrow street—what was it called?—reddened eyes searched for, found, failed to read a name-plaque covered by a fringe of icicles—a bus had skidded and rammed a wall. White-faced, teeth chattering from shock now as well as cold, its passengers were returning to the last stop to await a replacement. Passive, he stood watching from about thirty yards' distance.

—Fossils . . . Yes, this is like being a corpuscle inside a dying dinosaur. Half the street-lamps out. Cars abandoned. Buses running off the road. Not enough power to keep the underground trains on schedule. Gangrene is setting in.

At the thought of that, he reflexively touched his arm. Amazingly, though, it was healing well. It no longer hurt.

"Are you all right?" The question, kindly enough, from one of the frustrated bus-riders as he drew abreast: a man in a fur-fabric coat, worn at collar and cuffs, but still enviably warm.

"Me? Oh—yes, thanks. I'm okay."

"You don't look it! Standing out here in your shirt-sleeves, soaking . . . What you ought to do, chum, is go to St Sebastian's. They'll give you a cuppa and something to eat, and they may have a coat to spare." The man hesitated as though about to venture an obscenity. "That is, unless you—uh—take drugs? They don't let in addicts."

With a reassuring headshake: "Thank you. I didn't know about this. I'm pretty much a stranger in London."

"I can hear that. Canadian, aren't you? Well, just turn right at the end of this street, and . . ."

So he did, and found himself in a few minutes on the front steps of a pillared building declared by a big board to be CHURCH OF SAINT SEBASTIAN MARTYR. He climbed the steps, pushed open a heavy door of dark wood on iron-strap hinges.

A high roof. Empty chairs. Air marginally warmer than outside, not much. Candles burning distant on an altar backed by a stained-glass window depicting Sebastian the Human Pincushion in all his gory. Childhood image: a fakir drawn by Ripley, with *believe it or not* great spikes through arms and calves.

He walked slowly towards the eastern end.

"Here, you! What do you think you're doing?"

Emerging from a side-chapel, a portly florid dark-clad man, bustling and puffing with self-importance. And, taking in the shirt-sleeved soaking stubble-chinned stray: "Down the crypt, get along with you! Don't want you up here making a mess all over the place—we got a special service in the morning, and we only just cleaned up for it!"

There were wet smears from the door to where the snow-saturated shoes had halted.

But his flow of words broke off abruptly. The newcomer had looked at him, square in the eyes.

And now said, "I fell among thieves. But I'll let you pass by on the other side."

He walked away.

"Now—now just a second!" the portly man gasped, and came hurrying after. "I didn't mean to—!"

"But you did," the stranger said, and with a burst of angry energy hauled wide the heavy door and slammed it behind him with a crash that almost deafened the Pharisee.

—Thieves? True enough.

Three of them, while he had been hiding from pursuers barely less friendly. He had heard whispered words—"Look, he has his arm in a sling!"—and imagining sympathy had let them come up to him, and when they set about him it was impossible to fight back. They took his jacket containing his billfold, gagged him, tied his hands to his ankles with the sling, left him in the cold and wet to work free if he could.

It had taken time. It had been managed.

And, moneyless, he had gone exploring. Strange to this city, having visited it before but only on the luxury level, he had walked mile after freezing mile, staring in dismay—at lines of grey-faced housewives waiting for loaves a penny cheaper here than across the street; at children hobbling bandy-legged with rickets out of snow-white school playgrounds; at others who had scratched their scalps raw for the lice that infested them; at able-bodied men in groups of six or eight at street-corners, hands deep in pockets, shoulders hunched, coatless and down-at-heel, while sleet and scraps of litter blew around their legs.

At a Rolls-Royce whose indecent half-nude mascot had been replaced by a crucifix.

He had slept where tiredness overcame him, under the arches of an incomplete elevated road; it carried no traffic, so he was quiet there. On either side houses stood vacant, windows smashed and doors nailed or padlocked, signs warning that they were patrolled by guard-dogs. Curiously, he had not been cold, though his only covering had been a couple of sacks. But he ought to have eaten something. He could feel that he ought. That was a novel sensation, known as hunger. In thirty-four years he had scarcely missed a meal; there was always food in his world, at fixed times. Now, he realised, he was burning vast amounts of energy to keep warm. His muscles, his very bones were complaining, and he had had to draw his belt in a full inch.

Around the side of the church a sign said REFUGE and pointed down a flight of icy steps to the crypt. He descended, found a door, on pushing it open was assailed by the smell of old clothes, steaming tea, stale bread. In a dour line fifty men and women as shabby as himself and even grimier were awaiting sweet tea in enamel mugs, bread-rolls smeared with margarine, and the chance to sit down on benches already fully occupied, so that a young man in a black front and clerical collar was walking around saying, "If you've finished, *would* you make room for others, please?"

A man responded, near the door, letting fall a copy of *The Right Way*, the monthly journal published by the Campaign Against Moral Pollution. It must have passed through several hands, being torn and tea-stained. Seeing it would be long before he reached the head of the line, the new arrival picked it up and glanced through it. He had seen it before. Lady Washgrave had sent a copy to his home in California. The main feature was an article by the Right Honourable Henry Charkall-Phelps, PC, MP, fulminating against the decline in educational standards he claimed had overtaken Britain.

A paragraph containing a name leapt to his eye.

We would do better to copy the example of the government of Greece, cradle of Western culture. A godless and immoral corrupter of the young, like that so-called "teacher" Malcolm Fry whose foul influence fortunately came to light thanks to the selfless dedication of members of our Campaign . . .

"So if you wouldn't mind moving on—? Hey, I say! I didn't mean you, I meant people who've already been served!"

But the door was swinging shut.

It was seldom that Billy Cohen felt the need to patronise a gay club or gay bar. There were few of them left in London anyway; the palmy days of ten years ago when he had finally come to terms with his own nature and decided not to be ashamed of his inclinations had faded into wistful memory under the battering of the Puritan backlash. No question of legislation was involved—that remained theoretically very liberal. Just as passing laws had not stopped people drinking under Prohibition, though, it had not affected the fury of the bigots who, perhaps, were afraid of admitting to the same impulse in themselves. Bands of vigilantes patrolled Hampstead Heath and Wimbledon Common with dogs and water-pistols full of indelible dye; sometimes a young man was found dead with a cross carved on his forehead, though admittedly that had only happened three times in the three years since he moved to Britain permanently, thinking it less risky than New York on the basis of half a dozen short visits.

One after another, however, gay clubs and gay pubs were having their liquor-licences withdrawn on specious grounds, in every case as the result of a well-organised, well-financed campaign of local agitation. So few were left.

Tonight he felt for once that he must be in company where he could relax. Ruth had been given notice to quit the Civil Service, a terrible blow in these times of high unemployment, and—

—How can she have been so *cruel?*

He had finished helping Malcolm to clean up the wreck of Mary's room, the quiet devout girl lodging next to him who barely exchanged helloes in the morning before vanishing to work. She had become, without warning, hysterical, and had screamed that she could no longer live in the same house with a man who shamelessly kept a mistress, and boasted moreover that it had been she who informed on Ruth to her department's chief. And smashed the windows, and the mirror, and the lamps, and the china hand-basin, and stormed out calling down fire and brimstone.

Malcolm had taken it all philosophically enough. Even so . . .

—I'm going to ask Kneller if I can be a VC guinea-pig too. Mal's been transformed. He's suddenly confident. He breathes the impression that he's going to do something big, very soon. What? And will he get the chance? All this talk of war . . .

He shivered as he walked, not from cold. It was dreadfully convincing, that war idea, the way Malcolm argued it. Dalessandro's general strike had succeeded fantastically; the entire country had been brought to a halt for a full day. Now he was in the open, addressing public meetings where the response was as frenzied as in the time of Mussolini, whom he often invoked. If he took over, he promised, he would pull Italy out of the Common Market, reimpose high tariffs, close the frontiers to competing foreign goods . . . And the other countries in the Market wouldn't stand for it.

If war did follow, what could hinder it? He knew a little history; knew that in 1914 the international labour movement so many people had relied on to prevent open conflict had crumpled like wet paper under a wave of crazy nationalism; knew there had been self-sealing fuel-tanks marked "Made in USA" in the Messerschmitt 110 which Rudolf Hess flew to Scotland, epitaph on the aspirations of those who had struggled to stop the Nazis. And knew above all that the guilty had more often gone free than been condemned.

This time, there was no massive antiwar movement at all. The superpowers might even be glad of a European conflict to distract their people from local problems: in America, the black ghettos were exploding in winter instead of summer, measure of the desperate frenzy the workless underprivileged were feeling, while it was on the cards that the U.S.S.R. was about to reap the harvest of decades of bureaucratic inefficiency, commit troops ignominiously within its own borders as formerly in Budapest, Prague, East Berlin . . . and as another power had been compelled to do in Belfast a few years ago, in Glasgow recently.

Once you had been shown the path of the powder-train, it was hard not to believe that a spark would sooner or later light it.

Here he was, though, at his destination: a club of which he was not a member but where he could rely on finding an acquaintance willing to invite him in. It was a basement in a narrow alley to the north of Oxford Street whose manager by dint of incredible ingenuity had kept one step ahead of the Campaign Against Moral Pollution's attempts to close him down. He complied scrupulously with fire regulations, liquor laws, hygiene laws, never allowed noisy music to leak out that might cause neighbours to complain.

And never never advertised except on the grapevine.

As Billy had hoped, several friends of his were present, and one of them promptly signed him in as a guest. Relaxing, accepting the offer of a drink, he joined in the normal small-talk of the day: theatre-gossip, scandal, wishful thinking . . .

Almost an hour had gone by before there was an interruption. A loud bumping noise was heard from the front entrance: something heavy falling down the flight of steps that led to it. The duty barman and two customers hurried to see what had happened, and found the door jammed by the—the whatever. Their best efforts could not force it back more than three or four inches.

Alarm spread like a cold wind. The customers fell silent. One drew back a curtain and peered through a window.

"Godheads!" he screamed at the shrill top of his voice.

"What?"—from a dozen throats. And someone said, "Back way, quickly!"

At which same moment came a noise of hammering.

Billy was among those who reached the fire emergency exit first. Just in time to recognise the stench of kerosene being poured under the door—to lean against it with insane force and find that the nails newly driven into a bar across it were going to hold . . .

And a fiery cross came smashing through the window.

XVI

Braking his car outside number 25 Chater Street, Kneller muttered, "I never thought the day would come when I had to steal from my own labs!" Automatically he patted the bulge in his pocket where he carried a precious test-tube well protected with plastic foam and cotton-wool.

"I don't imagine Maurice did, either," Randolph said greyly. "After what Gifford let slip, though . . . Isn't it incredible? It's the kind of thing you read about in other countries, and smugly believe could never happen here."

"Exactly," Kneller said, locking the car. "And— Oh, we must have timed it perfectly. Isn't that Chief Inspector Sawyer?" He pointed at a dark-coated man favouring one foot as he climbed Malcolm's steps.

"So it is. Fantastic how he deduced what had happened to him, isn't it? And to think we had his name right in front of us and didn't make the connection!"

"Well, when he phoned he said he never uses the double-barrelled version . . . Ah, there's Malcolm opening the door. Come on."

A moment later, in the hallway, Malcolm was saying, "So you're the mysterious 'David Eric Jarman-Sawyer', are you?"

"I still don't know how you worked that out," Sawyer parried.

"We have a list," Malcolm murmured.

"Of people affected by VC, you mean? I'd like to see it!"

"So you shall. But wait a moment. There's someone in the living-room you ought to meet."

Puzzled, they followed him, and found Ruth—red-eyed as though she had been weeping—silently serving soup and bread to a lean man with a stubble of new beard seated at the breakfast-counter. Sawyer stopped dead.

"Brother Bradshaw!" he burst out.

"In person," Malcolm said, while Bradshaw set about the food as though he hadn't eaten in weeks and Ruth retired quietly to the far end of the room, where the TV with its sound low was showing a series of riots: Glasgow, Detroit, Tbilisi, Milan, in swift succession. "He found his way here for such a ridiculous reason, I can't help wondering whether VC may not be infinitely more powerful than we imagine. He spotted an article by Charkall-Phelps in *The Right Way* which called me a corrupter of youth, and having met Charkall-Phelps decided that anyone he hates as much as he hates me must be a decent type."

"It's more complicated than that," Bradshaw said, his mouth full of bread. "I went looking for refuge in a church, and a pompous guy ordered me out because I was dirtying the floor, and I kind of pulled the complete Jesus act on him, which blew his mind into tiny pieces. While my own mind was still running on the parable of the Good Samaritan—I'd told him I fell among thieves—I spotted Malcolm's name, like he said. Not for the first time, because they sent that issue of the magazine to help persuade me to join their Crusade. Being reminded of it, being here in a strange country where I know almost nobody, I thought, well, who is my neighbour? More likely him than these Pharisees and Sadducees! So I went looking for a phone-directory, and . . . here I am." He renewed his attack on the soup.

"Bless you, Charkall-Phelps," Malcolm murmured. "Do sit down, all of you—use the bed if there's nowhere else. Ruth dear, what about some wine for . . . ? Sorry." Turning to fetch a bottle and glasses himself. Over his shoulder: "I'm afraid Ruth got sacked today. Thanks to a bitch who was lodging here that I'm glad to see the back of . . . Oh, Chief Inspector, you wanted to see our list. I'll give it to you."

Sawyer said, "About to be ex-chief inspector. I've put in my resignation." And without bothering to explain, seized the computer print-out.

"Bott! That's Harry Bott! No wonder he was able to shop so many villains to me! And . . . Incredible. I know them all."

"Crawford?" Malcolm rapped, distributing glasses of wine to Kneller and Randolph.

"Yes, he's been in trouble with the school attendance officer. Runs a black power study-group that keeps kids away from regular schooling. I can give you his address if you like."

"And Stevens too? Just by reputation?"

"No, personally. I arrested him when he was about seventeen. He was running with a gang of bloody-minded yobboes. Got probation. But he's dead now, you know."

"What?"

"Yes, they cancelled the deserter's warrant they had out for him this afternoon. It'll be in the news tonight, I expect." Vaguely waving at the TV. "You know he walked out of hospital with his wounds unhealed? Well, he caught an antibiotic-resistant infection and it gangrened. When they found him he was delirious with toxaemia. Not a hope of saving his life."

He checked. "You heard that? I said 'delirious with toxaemia'! A week or two ago I'd have had to look that up in the dictionary!"

"Typical," Kneller said after a brief hesitation.

"How can you be sure? Don't answer that, I know this VC stuff can produce amazing effects. Now I've met Mr Fry, for example, I recall an assault case involving a Mr Cohen of this address which should have led, but didn't, to a charge of assault with a deadly weapon, and happened the day after Dr Post was killed and furthermore on blood-donation day at the Lister Clinic. Mr Fry, were you the man Post showed off his pills to?"

"Yes."

"And you took one, and gave blood . . . ? *I* see! So everybody who has VC caught it the way Harry and I did, through plasma?"

Kneller drew a deep breath. "That list isn't complete any

longer. Dr Post had it. I have it. Dr Randolph has it. We carried out tests, and they proved positive."

"Anybody else—?" Sawyer began, and was interrupted by a sudden sob from Ruth, who, unnoticed, had buried her face in her hands.

In astonishment Malcolm turned, poised to hurry over and comfort her . . . and halted, staring. He said faintly, "Wilfred, it just hit me. I asked about supportive media for VC."

"Yes, and I have news for you on that front. Arthur and I think we've come up with a medium superior to what Maurice designed, and so simple you can literally cook it on a kitchen stove. It's a breakthrough like using brewer's wastes to grow *penicillium notatum*—"

"Shut up!" Malcolm ordered, clenching his fists. "*Saliva?*"

And at that moment the doorbell rang.

"I'll go," Ruth said, wearily rising. "It's Dr Campbell. I recognise his walk, even though I've met him exactly twice. Yes, Malcolm. That must be how it happened, through kissing you— No, don't touch me! I'm still shaking deep inside. I only realised today, and I feel so . . ."

The words trailed away in her wake.

And a moment later Hector rushed into the room, waving a sheet of paper. "Malcolm—Wilfred—listen to this! Hello!" On realising other people were present. "Chief Inspector! What in . . . ? Never mind, listen to what I have here. It's Ministry of Health Procedural Directive eighty-oblique-oh-five, and it instructs hospitals to double the payment to blood-donors and stockpile the maximum quantity of plasma!"

Kneller's jaw dropped. But before anyone could speak Ruth clicked shut the door, having regained her composure, and said in a near-normal voice, "I'm sorry to be such a fool. It's just that coming on top of everything else it was a hell of a shock. Not so bad as what you went through, Malcolm, because my case must be more like Wilfred and Arthur's. I suppose I've been sleeping half an hour longer per night . . . But the tension! Oh, it's dreadful!"

"I don't understand!" Hector cried.

"It would appear," Kneller said harshly, "that VC *is* loose in the world. Running wild, the way we suspected. But . . . Bluntly, the question is: wild *enough?*"

Bradshaw spoke up unexpectedly. "I think we should hold a council of war. I mean that literally. I only heard about this VC stuff when I met Malcolm tonight, but—well, I've been through what it can do to a man, and it's fantastic."

All eyes turned on him as he left the breakfast-counter and came to join them.

"I don't imagine any of you have been aboard a nuclear submarine equipped with MIRV-Poseidons?" he went on. "I have. A college friend of mine captains one, and invited me to preside at her launching, and later when she was commissioned took me to sea to witness a full-dress rehearsal for hostilities. At the time I was thrilled, of course. I didn't realise what I was watching: proof that there are people in the world willing and able to destroy mankind."

There followed a chill pause, almost total but for the very faint sound from the TV.

Bradshaw glanced at Kneller. "I know what you mean when you ask 'wild enough?' In my case, and I hope this is some reassurance to you, ma'am"—with a glance at Ruth—"VC has done a lot of good. Mr Sawyer, I gather you are, or were, a detective?"

Sawyer nodded.

"Can you imagine what it's been like for me, wearing one of the best-known faces on earth, to remain anonymous when everybody and his uncle was hunting for me? I did it. I was never much good as an actor—I traded on my looks—but I was trained by one of the finest coaches in Hollywood, and things he taught me years ago have come real in my mind. I swear I could meet my wife on the sidewalk and she wouldn't give me a second glance."

"You've had no undesirable side-effects?" Kneller demanded.

"Sure I have." Bradshaw grimaced. "It's no fun to discover that you've let other people do your thinking for you all your life, is it? Me, I've always leaned on a psychological crutch: in school and college, then the Army, then with the agent who got me my part in *Gunslinger*, then the church . . . But I finally learned how to stand up and think for myself."

Sawyer was very pale. He said, "Isn't it hell? I . . . Oh, I have at least three murders on my conscience. Killings I had the data to prevent, only I didn't work out in time what was going on."

Sweat stood out on his face. "I thought until today I was getting my chance to make amends, thanks to VC. I've been assembling a dossier on a property developer who used frighteners to evict people illegally from their homes, and made a fortune as a result. He's out of reach, but the money is still around, and it's an old principle of common law that a criminal shall not profit by his crime. But today I was called to the Home Office and told that if I persist I can look forward to a faked medical discharge. He didn't just break the law, that bastard, he smashed it and danced on the bits! And because the Home Secretary is a friend of the person who inherited . . . Well, that's why I've sent in my resignation. I'm sick of it all."

"I imagine you're talking about Sir George Washgrave," Malcolm said.

Sawyer blinked. "You don't sound very surprised!"

"Should I be? I taught some of the kids whose families he evicted from buildings near here." Malcolm turned to a chair, kicked it around as though it had injured him, and sat down, reaching to take Ruth's hand. But she avoided him.

"I know people like that in the States," Bradshaw said. "Bleed the poor in slum tenements, salve their consciences with gifts to charity . . . But—Mr Campbell! Or is it Doctor?"

Hector, who had been more and more at a loss as the conversation developed, said mechanically, "Doctor."

"I take it you think this directive about stockpiling plasma is a precaution against war?"

"Uh . . . Well, I can't be sure. It just seems likely."

"It's more than likely," Kneller said. "As some of you know, our Institute is plagued with government investigators evaluating VC. In charge of them is a smooth devil named Gifford. Something he said today, in a fit of bad temper, scared Arthur and me out of our wits."

"He accused us both of being traitors," Randolph said. "Hampering him when, if it weren't for him and the other people who are loyal to Charkall-Phelps, nobody would be taking any steps to help Britain survive the coming war."

"He said that, in so many words?" Malcolm took a pace forward, and the others gasped in dismay.

"In so many words," Kneller confirmed.

"That figures," Bradshaw said. "World War Three is going to start in Europe, same as the other two did. I believe I can tell you why. I—uh—I did take a degree in theology, you know. I'm not just an unqualified self-appointed evangelist. I mean I wasn't. That's behind me. Same as with everything else in my life, though, I approached what I learned with eyes and ears half-closed. It's only now I realise how dangerous and destructive Christian culture has become. If there was ever any love in it, it's been bled out. Three major religions preach Holy War: Shinto, Islam, and Christianity. Christianity is the only one hypocritical enough simultaneously to enjoin its followers to turn the other cheek and suffer fools gladly and the rest of it. Look at the record. Germany was a Christian country almost exactly one hundred times as long as it was Nazi. Did the Nazis undo in twelve years all the church had done in twelve centuries? No, they built on it. Hitler was a baptised Catholic and never excommunicated. When he was enlisting the support of the bishops in 1933 he promised to do nothing to the Jews that the church had not done already, and kept his promise. Which is why the clergy turned over their parish records so that converts with Jewish ancestry could be identified and killed."

"That's not fair!" Ruth burst out. "They weren't all—"

"For every Niemöller," Bradshaw snapped, "there were a thousand who collaborated. And even Niemöller was an ex-U-boat captain, a willing professional murderer!"

"I—uh—I'd forgotten," Ruth muttered, and added almost inaudibly, "But I can't forget anything any more . . ."

"Did Gifford say"—from Malcolm—"the people at your lab are personally loyal to Charkall-Phelps?"

"Yes, he did," Kneller sighed. "It's of a piece with his career in politics, I suppose: business background, safe seat, Home Office within ten years where he can control the police . . . I was saying to Arthur as we arrived, the kind of thing you imagine can't happen here. Plus an enormous populist movement handed to him on a plate, the Moral Pollution Campaign whose members are desperately seeking a scapegoat for what's actually due to government incompetence, like high prices and bad housing and unemployment. I suspect he's after a monopoly of VC. It would be the very thing he needs to secure personal supreme power in the chaos caused by the coming war."

"Which, we are agreed, will be triggered off in Italy," Randolph said, and added dryly, "Capital—Rome!"

Bewildered, Ruth said, "How is it you're always in agreement? Is the result of VC going to be that everyone on earth will think alike? We might as well be ants!"

"Let's ask Hector's opinion," Malcolm said. "If Billy were home I'd call him in too, but he's not. Hector, right here we have all but two of the people known to be infected with VC. There were two others, but both are dead. I say the consequences of taking VC have been good in my case. I can organise data more efficiently, and on levels I never before had the chance to react on. And you know I'm physically healthy."

Hector nodded. "Granted. Uh—Wilfred, what about you?"

"I'm doing work at the labs, or could be but for those damned meddlers, which I'd never have expected. It's a cliché that a scientist does no original work after thirty. Maurice disproved that, and now Arthur and I are doing the same."

"As for me," Bradshaw said, "I have no reservations about VC. I've suffered . . . but it's the right kind of suffering. I feel purified."

"David?" Malcolm looked at Sawyer. "Oh, excuse me. It's the blood-brother bit, as it were."

"I don't mind. It's the same with me. Obviously I have an aptitude for detection, or I wouldn't have made chief inspector. But these past few days I've been solving, in my head, cases five, six, seven years old." He hesitated. "Moreover I've watched Harry Bott grow a conscience. Small-time thief, practising Catholic, treated his wife abominably. Now he says he's going to go straight. I believe him."

"But what about Corporal Stevens?" Ruth cried. "Caught trying to send a parcel-bomb to his officer's wife? What about this man Crawford who runs a black power group? What about his opposite number in South Africa who's spent his life sopping up so-called proofs that black people are subhuman? You can't calculate with data you don't possess!"

"I think," Malcolm said slowly, "our minds have been made up for us. Sorry, Hector." He pointed at the TV, whose screen showed the single word NEWSFLASH, and turned up the volume.

A voice said, "—regular programmes to bring you this important announcement. The northern frontiers of Italy have been closed since an hour ago, and both radio and television have ceased transmission. It can be confidently assumed that as a result of his successful strike call last Monday Marshal Dalessandro—"

"Did you know," Malcolm said at random, "that they're advertising the army again on Radio Free Enterprise? Owing to the record unemployment, recruiting figures have been high for months. Do I hear anybody say 'waste of public money'?"

The TV voice said: "—mobilisation in Switzerland . . ."

"That does it," Randolph said. "Nobody could fail to be aware what another war would mean. Not since 1945. But it's clear that it's possible to disregard that knowledge."

"I've met people who can," Bradshaw said.

"Yes. Well, what VC does is make it more difficult to ignore data you possess, right? So it's our duty to turn this outbreak of VC into an epidemic. There simply isn't any other way to save the world."

He glanced at Kneller. "Wilfred?"

The professor felt in his pocket, produced the packet which made it bulge, and began carefully to unwrap it.

"We have the means," he said. "This, for your information, is what VC looks like in the unpurified state." He held up a sealed glass cylinder full of a yellowish mass with red veins running through it. "There's enough here to affect five or six hundred people. With luck, in a month we could multiply that by a thousand. But we may not have a month. We shall just have to do the best we can."

"First reactions from Brussels . . ." said the TV.

"But you have no right!" Ruth cried. "People ought to have the chance to choose!"

"So they should," Malcolm countered sternly. "But how many of us will be given the choice whether or not to die in World War Three?"

BOOK THREE

Dissent

"An atheist could not be as great a military leader as one who is not an atheist. . . . I don't think you will find an atheist who has reached the peak in the Armed Forces."

—Admiral Thomas H. Moorer,
when chairman-designate of
the Joint Chiefs of Staff,
quoted in the *Milwaukee Journal*

XVII

There was silence. Malcolm made it more complete by switching off the TV.

"Ruth," he said in a tone suddenly full of tenderness, "it would clear all our consciences, not just yours, if we could persuade Hector what we plan to do is right. That's what I had in mind when I appealed to him just now. I submit to you that one could not at random pick a more ideal judge. He is not affected by VC, but he knows about it, and he knows people who have it, and he has examined one of them—me—using tests of his own choice and all available medical facilities. Furthermore, he is a doctor in general practice at a large clinic. Not only is he acquainted with the use of virtually every drug in the pharmacopoeia; he is also acquainted with the social conditions that obtain in London today, because he sees patients from every class every day. It's a dreadful burden to place on any man. But if he is willing to undertake the task, will you abide by what he says?"

Stiff-featured and pale, Ruth countered, "Will the rest of you? Or will you simply go ahead anyway?"

"If we can't prove to you and Hector that it's right, it won't be worth doing. Particularly to you."

"What? Why?" She stared at him.

"Because you were deprived of your own life, and that hasn't made you hate the world. You care about it, and the people in it. It would be pointless reasoning with somebody like Charkall-Phelps, who doesn't give a damn for mankind, only for himself."

"And if we can't persuade you," Kneller said, "I'll personally destroy this." He held up the test-tube.

"Good. Hector?"

"You want me to—to sort of interrogate you about your motives, is that it? I'll do my best, although . . ." Hector gathered himself. "Very well! To begin with, all my instincts as a doctor cry out against turning loose VC, a substance that once at large can never be eradicated short of killing everybody who carries it. Maurice asked me whether someone who had it in his power to alter human nature should do so. I couldn't answer. I still can't. Such a thing is unprecedented."

"Not at all," Malcolm said. "It's directly owing to just such a chemical alteration in a large terrestrial population that we can sit here and reason with one another." He glanced at Kneller. "Wilfred, you must know what I'm talking about."

"I believe I do. The loss of the enzyme which converts urea to allantoin."

"I don't know about that," Ruth said stubbornly. "Or"—seemingly suddenly giddy, she put her hands to her temples—"or do I? It's so awful, this turnover period! Neither able to remember nor able to forget!"

"Urea stimulates activity in the nervous system," Malcolm said. "Loss of the power to excrete it as allantoin has been compared to adding a permanent pep-pill to our diet."

"I—uh . . . Yes, I read about it once. But in a story. Not an article or a book that I'd have taken seriously." Ruth let her hands fall to her lap.

"But that occurred naturally," Hector objected. "What you're planning is—"

Malcolm interrupted. "Are we not natural creatures? Are we not evolved, too? Surely all the lessons we've learned in the past century come to a single point: we have to stop thinking of ourselves as somehow apart from nature, and recognise that we're inseparable from it."

"Which is something I'm keenly aware of," Randolph said. "Since catching VC I feel that instead of being an isolated entity which I keep here in my frontal lobes"—tapping his forehead—"my consciousness is more integrated with the rest of me. The forebrain has been termed a tumourous outgrowth, and inasmuch as a tumour has the power to kill that's an apt comparison. Thanks to it, we've become able to ruin the world we live in and even to exterminate our species. Rationally, that's a decision we ought never to take. But if it is taken it won't be on a rational basis."

"Inside my head," Malcolm quoted, "a man is trying to ride a dog which is trying to ride a lizard. We find it easy to decide which way we'd like to go. Because we're being pulled three ways at once, small wonder we never get there!"

"And small wonder," Bradshaw chimed in, "that so many of us give up—cast ourselves on the mercy of a hypothetical all-powerful supreme being who can really do what we can only envisage."

"We all know what it's like to have plans frustrated," Ruth said, and gave a slight shudder. Clearly she was struggling to control herself. "That's among the reasons why we sometimes lose our tempers and strike out at random and even kill one another. But it's an inescapable part of being human."

"What we're saying," Malcolm contradicted, "is that it isn't inescapable any longer. Consider. Plans can be frustrated by inanimate forces, and it's foolish to rail against them. If a thunderstorm blows tiles off your roof and your home gets flooded, you may be angry but you don't blame the storm. On the other hand you have every reason to blame the builder who last mended the roof if he charged you a fat fee for making it stormproof. The weather is beyond reach of a complaint. Other human beings aren't. What hurts is to have your plans frustrated by people whom you think of as being trustworthy because they're members of your species."

"Wait a moment," Hector said. "I was describing to Wilfred the other day how some of my Irish patients expect me to cure with a single pill children who are mentally disturbed because they had to live through years of violence at home." He leaned back in his chair. "I can't help letting them down. What they expect of me is literally out of the question."

"Don't you tell them so?" Malcolm said.

"Of course, but they don't listen."

"VC makes it impossible not to listen," Malcolm murmured. "If they had VC, those people would stop treating you like a magician and start treating you like a doctor."

"Exactly," Kneller agreed. "They'd be able to draw on their own and other people's experience of what medicine is. They no doubt have the information, and they disregard it."

"But merely making use of more information isn't a panacea," Hector snapped, reverting to his devil's advocate rôle. "While I'm not a hundred per cent convinced you've made your point about this being analogous to what's already happened in the course of evolution, I do have to concede that the chance of another war breaking out does seem very real, and what with nuclear weapons that's like writing a factor of infinity into an equation. Admitting something has to be done, the question stands: is this the right thing to do? Could the ability to calculate with all the data accumulated in a lifetime help a savage in—oh—New Guinea if fallout came sifting down and everyone in the village was ill with radiation sickness?"

"Yes," Malcolm said promptly. "Given that people had been weak and ill before and some had recovered when they did this or that or the other, ate this or that, drank this or that . . . You picked a poor example; radiation sickness has to be cured by helping the body to mend itself."

"Besides, we're not talking about New Guinea savages," Sawyer said. "We're talking about technological Western man. Here's a question for you, Doctor. Do you approve of murder, the pushing of hard drugs, and driving people out of their homes with dogs and petrol-bombs?"

"What? No, of course I don't."

"As to driving people out of their homes, it's because Harry Bott caught VC that the memory of his spell as a frightener has turned him against crime for good. As to drug-peddling, VC persuaded him to shop his brother-in-law Joe Feathers, whom we'd been after for years without success. As to murder, but for catching VC myself I couldn't have deduced just by looking at Dr Post's body that I very probably already had his killer under arrest. Nor could I have assembled that dossier on Washgrave Properties. How did George Washgrave get away with it? He exploited our selective inattention." Glancing at Kneller and Randolph. "I didn't know that term until I heard it from you at Post's home. But that's what he took advantage of. He was a filthy villain, but he was rich and respectable and gave to charity and went to church every Sunday, and that's what people took notice of."

"Which brings us to the nub of the matter," Malcolm said. "How do you fool people? How do you get them to put up with things that are harmful to them and bring you a handsome profit? How do you get them to eat food that doesn't nourish them properly? How do you get them to believe it's worth emptying serviceable houses at a time of shortage in order to build a motorway that the homeless citizens can't afford to use?" He pointed in the direction of the one which droned day and night within earshot of Chater Street. "How do you get them to re-elect you to power when you've made ghastly mistakes and propose to keep right on repeating them? As it were, 'We did it before and it didn't work but it damned well should have done so let us do it again!' We're seeing that around us all the time: the cost of living doubled in the past four years, the number of unemployed doubled too, and services *halved!* Lord, street-lamps switched off, tube-trains packed to overload capacity, the Health Service being cut back, people suffering from scurvy and rickets in one of the world's richest countries! How do you get away with it? Above all, how do you persuade people to risk their lives in order to kill total strangers whom they know almost literally nothing about? Why, the answer's simple. You lie to them!"

He leaned forward earnestly. "And all too often the lie is easier to believe than the truth."

"I've used that technique," Bradshaw said. "You said a moment ago, Malcolm, that Dr Campbell's patients look on him as more of a magician. Magic is what movements like the Moral Pollution Campaign are based on. The argument runs like this: we've misbehaved and so we're being punished. We must seek out the wicked atheists and perverts and deal with them, and when we've demonstrated that we hate their guts everything will be all right again."

"You can find magic in the law, too," Sawyer said. "It's used to cover up every conceivable type of inconsistency. If you kill a dozen people by sniping at them from a roof-top, you're a criminal. Unless you had a uniform on. Then you get a medal. That's more or less what Corporal Stevens said when he created that terrific scandal on TV in Scotland—and he was quite right. I arrested him when he was running with that gang I told you about, for doing what he was ordered to do in Glasgow!"

"Our whole society is schizophrenic from top to bottom," Malcolm said.

"Absolutely!" Kneller snapped. "But it's not surprising when you're being asked to lick the boots of the people who are simultaneously either beating or starving you into submission!"

"I still don't see," Hector declared doggedly, "how VC can cure us. What we need is an injection of raw empathy. That might do some good. Not extra knowledge. Extra—ah—love!"

"That will come of its own accord," Malcolm said. "Will you grant that human beings are readily frightened by what they don't understand? And that when they're afraid they can more easily be manipulated?"

"Ah . . . Yes, of course."

"Will you further grant that they are most commonly manipulated by propaganda, which is a kind of lying?"

"Yes." Hector looked uncomfortable, as though he felt he was being pushed towards a conclusion he didn't relish.

"Will you concede that a population in full possession of data from past experience will, when invited to go and commit publicly sanctioned mass murder at the risk of their own lives, remember the faults and shortcomings of the leaders who are issuing the orders? Remember, for example, that they are the people who couldn't arrange a decent diet for them, or decent homes, or regular work, or proper medical care?"

"Just a—"

"I hadn't quite finished. Likewise will realise that they don't know anything about the so-called enemy *except what those known-to-be-untrustworthy leaders have told them?*"

Into the dead pause that followed, the ring of the phone in the hallway stabbed like a dagger.

"I'll go," Ruth said, rising quickly. "I—uh . . . You just keep on at Hector. I'm leaving it to him, as I said."

And she hastened from the room, closing the door behind her.

"You're taking too much for granted!" Hector snapped. "According to what I've been told, a general who's taken VC will become a better general. Like Ruth's South African. If all the data you possess tend to a particular view of the world—"

"But they don't. They can't," Malcolm said.

"Surely they can! Someone who's spent his whole life in isolation . . ." Hector hesitated. "Oh, I believe I see what you mean. Nobody can remain that isolated and still be human."

"Precisely. Your Afrikaner can't avoid being aware that there are people in the world who disagree with him about *Apartheid*. Your general in the Pentagon can't avoid being aware that there are people who seem perfectly happy under Communism, while there are others who apparently hate living under American free enterprise. Data available and power to do damage run in tandem; the people in the best-informed countries are also those who can create most havoc. Savages in New Guinea can't exterminate mankind and very probably couldn't conceive the idea of doing so. Citizens of the nuclear powers—"

The door swung open, and there was Ruth again, very pale. She said, "Does anybody here know a Mr Billy Cohen?"

They stared at her, not speaking.

"Because if anybody does," she went on, a high thin note of near-hysteria keening her voice, "they wouldn't know him now!"

"What's happened?" Malcolm leapt to his feet.

"That was the police. They found his wallet only partly burned." She walked forward very slowly, eyes fixed on nothing. "He was at a club called the Universal Joint. Have you heard about it? I have. Near Oxford Street. It was attacked by godheads this evening and set on fire. Seven people have been burned to death."

She was face to face with Malcolm now, her fists clenched, her eyes still not focused on anything in present time.

"Go ahead. Don't waste any more time arguing. If people could do that to Billy, they could do it to the whole wide world, and they wouldn't ask my permission any more than they asked his."

XVIII

Valentine Crawford had a TV set again. It had suddenly occurred to him that a trained repairman could find and fix up a set that nobody else wanted. So far as helping to keep Toussaint amused was concerned, he was kicking himself for not having thought of it before. So far as the window it opened for him on the world was concerned . . .

A smooth-cheeked young BBC interviewer was saying, "Marshal, it's a great honour for us to be the first foreign newsservice permitted to question you about your policies!"

To which a snort from Marshal Dalessandro, heavy-set, going bald, wearing civilian clothes of course, framed by the tricolour Italian flag.

"First of all, I'd like to ask whether you don't think that by closing your frontiers with other Common Market countries—"

Dalessandro interrupted. "We the people of Italy have been cheated and lied to about the Common Market. It was a confidence trick. With it has been stolen our national pride. To be made into mongrel beggars is disgusting to a person of honour."

"I'm not sure I—"

"So recently as the week before Christmas in London was a demonstration of Italians bribed to England by promises of good work and high wages, left unemployed and so poor not to pay their fare home. Who would not complain? But as they did speak out, a man drove a car into the meeting of them, and broke a man's legs, and was hardly punished."

"If I know the case you're talking about, he was convicted and—"

"And fined twenty pounds!" Dalessandro snapped. "Pounds?

What are pounds these days? It is to say no more than twenty francs, or twenty marks! More than that, too: have they not lured Italians to Germany with the same lies, and sent them home by force when they were not any longer wanted there?"

"It's true that the foreign labour-force in Germany has been somewhat overlarge these past few—"

"Excuses! We in Italy are sickened of excuses!" Dalessandro barked. "What they wanted was cheap labour. When it stopped being cheap, they changed their minds. They lied!"

"But given the degree to which the Italian economy has been integrated into the rest of Europe, are you not worried by the fact that the West German government in particular has said it won't stand for what you've done? And the French have adopted the same attitude. Millions of—uh—of kilos of French farm-produce, for example, are spoiling at the frontier stations which you closed when you imposed your new protective tariffs."

"There has been wild talk of reopening our frontiers by arms. Let them try. Let them only try!" Dalessandro leaned forward. "We the people of Italy have discovered again our pride. With God's help"—he crossed himself—"we shall guard it against all comers. No matter the cost, in life itself. We are decided."

He sat back and set his jaw defiantly.

"Cissy!" Valentine said.

"Yes, honey?" Prompt, she came and leaned over the back of his chair, putting her arms around his neck and kissing the top of his head. For an instant a pang of old doubt assailed him: having her live here with him, the reaction of the neighbours . . .

—The hell with 'em! She's a better wife for me at sixteen, and a better mother for Toussaint, than the other ever was! And if she likes it, and her mother likes it—well!

"Cis, I think them stinking buckras gon' kill us all."

"What?" She drew back and came around the chair to his side, staring. "But you been planning all these clever schemes to fix 'em! You got a dozen of 'em nailed to rights by their own laws!" She pointed at a stack of paper on the table in the middle of the room. Since returning from hospital, he had reviewed several past incidents where at the time he had thought there was no case to be brought under the Race Relations Act, but now saw how a charge could be made to stick. It was as though his repeated reading of that and related legislation had all by itself turned him into a lawyer.

"So what's the use of fixing 'em one by one when they're lining up for a world war?" he rapped.

"You—you joking!" she said, appalled.

"No, I can read it plain as a newspaper. It goes this way. Them French and Germans say they won't stand for the Italian take-over. The Italians say shit on *you!* So they try and push through with guns, and the Italians fight back. And the Italians in America say, we got to get in on the Italian side, and the Germans over there say hell, no. So we got two camps lining up. Now the Americans don't like the French, so they send their carriers and battleships to support the Italians. Anyhow they want to break up the Common Market 'cause it's an economic rival for them. Meantime the Russians see this big rich capitalist bloc doing all the things it says in their creed must happen to it, like quarrelling over the loot. So they move into Yugoslavia like they did in East Germany and Hungary because they see their way to carving off a chunk or two of where the local Communist Parties are strong, like the big industrial cities, and—"

"Man, you going too fast for me!" Cissy complained. "I don't know about all these here economic forces." She hesitated. "Matter of fact, I guess you been talking too much about that in class since you got home. Like we only had five today, right? 'Stead of ten or fifteen!"

"But it's important!" Valentine clenched his fists. "I'm explaining how there's going to be a nuclear war!"

Into the brief pause that followed broke the shrill yammer of the doorbell. She rose, sighing.

"Man, you surely have changed since that buckra cut you up. If this goes on . . ."

And, unlatching the door: "Yes?"

A strange voice answered. "Is Mr Valentine Crawford at home?"

"Ah . . . Who are you?"

"He doesn't know me, but . . . I'll be damned! Cissy Jones!"

Valentine jumped to his feet and hurried in Cissy's wake. As he came up to her, she said in amazement, "Why, Mr Fry! I was in your class when I was—uh—eleven, twelve!"

There stood a white man with a brown beard, smiling at her.

"Hey, this here's one of my old teachers!" Cissy went on, turning to Valentine. "He's the one they sacked 'cause he talked back at the man from Moral Pollution—I told you about him."

"May I come in?" Malcolm said, and Cissy hastily stood aside. The weather was once more bitter; the forecasters said it would continue like this until April or even possibly May.

After which there was much bustle of chairs being moved and Toussaint being shown off—better, though still coughing a lot at night—and tea being made and . . .

"Mr. Crawford, I see you were watching the TV news just now," Malcolm said eventually. "I presume they included the interview with Marshal Dalessandro which they used in the early-evening bulletin?"

Valentine gave a wary nod.

"What do you think of the situation?"

"Won't make too much difference what I think, in the long run," Valentine said. "I'll be dead. So will you, which I guess is a consolation. And him, and the rest of you."

"Honey—" Cissy began in agitation. Malcolm cut her short.

"Don't worry, Cissy. I entirely agree with Mr Crawford. The chance of war hasn't been so extreme since nineteen thirty-eight. And this time there are likely to be very few pieces left for the survivors to pick up."

"He's been saying the same," Cissy acknowledged.

"I'm not surprised," Malcolm said. "So, unless I'm much mistaken, he's an ideal person to help us prevent it."

"Prevent it?" Valentine echoed with scorn. "Not a hope! You buckras are built for killing, that's all you're good for. You're the ones who fight world wars, and we're the poor buggers who get slaughtered!" He grimaced. "Might not be a bad idea to let you get on with it. The people most likely to survive would be my people, and we'd make a better world than you've done."

Casting his eye around the room, Malcolm spotted a paperback and shot out his arm. "Are you saying Chaka Zulu was less bloodthirsty than Napoleon or Bismarck? Chaka, who stood in the door of his hut at the beginning of every year and ordered his impis to ravage a season's journey in whatever direction he cast his spear?"

Disconcerted, Valentine said, "You—uh—you studied up on Chaka?"

"I had a lot of black kids in my class. Like Cissy. I thought I ought to be able to tell them about African history as well as the Battle of Trafalgar and the Wars of the Roses!"

"That's a fact, Val," Cissy put in. "We all liked him a lot, Mr Fry, because he could answer questions like about Africa and places."

"Ah . . . Okay, Mr Fry. I'm glad to hear it. Makes you pretty much of an exception! But what's all this about being able to stop the next war?"

Malcolm explained.

"In times of trial," said the Right Honourable Henry Charkall-Phelps from the screen of the TV in Lady Washgrave's drawing-room—which when not in use could be disguised as an elegant commode in the gracious style of Queen Anne's reign—"the British people have never failed to respond with magnificent determination and unquenchable resolve. One can only hope that if this crisis does develop further, it will not prove to be the case that the dilution of our culture which we have sadly had to endure, the injection from abroad of traditions which are foreign to us, one can only hope that these forces will not prove to have weakened our glorious heritage. Speaking for

myself, while I did indeed have misgivings a short time ago,
I have been wonderfully reassured by recent events. In
particular, I'm comforted and given new hope by the splendid
response we've seen to the New Year's Crusade organised
by the Campaign Against Moral Pollution . . . of which as you
know I'm a patron. No more convincing gage could have been
given to the world of our determination to sacrifice mere sensory gratification in favour of those higher and more admirable
aims which in periods of open conflict are the sole justification for what we do: patriotism, love of freedom, and national
honour!"

"How true!" sighed Lady Washgrave, clasping her hands.
"How very true! And how well put, moreover . . . Oh, dear!"
As the chimes of the front doorbell intruded. "Tarquin, be
so kind if you please as to see who that is and state that I am
not at home!"

But Tarquin was already on his way.

"You seem, Home Secretary, to be taking the present European crisis somewhat more seriously than the majority of your
colleagues," ventured the TV interviewer. "Last night when
the Prime Minister addressed that meeting in—"

"One does receive the impression," Charkall-Phelps broke in,
"that certain persons take nothing seriously at all. It could
well be argued, in my view, that a nation lacking strong lead-
ership can scarcely be regarded as a nation."

He smiled frostily. "However, kindly do not attempt to lead
me into a discussion of that nature. For myself, I have every
confidence in the people of Britain."

"Thank you, Home Secretary," the interviewer said, and
spun his chair to face another camera. "Well, I have to confess
that I wasn't expecting such a forthright declaration from Mr
Charkall-Phelps! Over in our other studio we have a group of
journalists who—"

Lady Washgrave used the remote control on the arm of her
chair to cut off the sound as Tarquin re-entered the room.

"Who was it at the door?" she demanded. "And—and what
is that package you are carrying?"

He held up for her inspection an oblong box, flimsily wrapped in tissue which the rain had soaked; it was just over thawing-point tonight, and the wind was carrying what felt like half the ocean aloft.

Through the wrapping, a brand-name and a chart of enticing candies could be discerned.

"It was a—uh—a young *coloured* girl, milady," Tarquin said. "Accompanied by her little brother, a boy of about six, I'd estimate. A most sweet and well-mannered child, very disappointed when I said you were not at home."

He proffered an envelope on which the name "Lady Washgrave", ink-written, had run in blue tears.

"Possibly this note will explain the purpose of their visit?"

"Ah . . . Yes, of course." But as she took it, she kept casting nervous glances at the box. It was so easy to disguise a bomb in a small container nowadays, and one was aware that certain dissident elements . . . including coloured ones . . .

She read rapidly, and her mind changed on the instant. "Oh, Tarquin, listen to this! It touches my heart! The handwriting of course is not of the most legible, but . . . Well, one must make allowances, must one not? And certainly even if the doctrinal content of the cults which such people adhere to is questionable, there's little doubt of their sincerity. The letter says, 'Dear My Lady Washgrave'—isn't that sweet?—'We think what you're doing with your Crusade is wonderful and Mam says it's all right if me and my brother give you these sweeties. God bless you and amen, love from Cissy!'"

Tarquin beamed. "How delightful! And they must have gone to so much trouble, too. I'm well aware that these are your preferred brand of sweets, but in view of your reluctance to associate yourself with commercial advertising it must have been remarkable insight which enabled the little girl to make such a correct choice."

He was peeling off the outer wrappings as he spoke.

For one last heartbeat Lady Washgrave felt a pang of alarm. There were certain associations connected with this make of candy. Whenever the late Sir George wished to put her in a mood to tolerate his—ah—animal urges, he had invariably prefaced the evening with a gift of just such a box as this one. Or rather, the large size, containing not half a kilo but a full kilo . . .

Then Tarquin was extending the open box for her to make a selection.

"It does occur to me," he murmured, "that since no reference is made in the note to a male parent, they may well be fatherless . . . I do wish you had seen them, milady. The little boy in particular was charming, like a walking doll."

"Oh, indeed, they can be delightful," Lady Washgrave conceded. She popped a red sweet into her mouth, and poised her hand undecided between a blue and a yellow one to follow. "If it were not for the work of agitators, who infect them with dreams they are simply not equipped to accomplish . . ."

She picked up the yellow one, on reflection. And said, "Perhaps you would like one also, Tarquin?"

"Thank you, milady."

He took the blue one.

But she finished all the others herself before retiring.

XIX

"I think all this is fantastic," Sawyer said, leaning on the breakfast-counter in Malcolm's living-room and watching as his host checked over the ordinary gallon-size wine-jars in which—thanks to the new supportive medium—VC was being bred at an incredible rate. There were advantages to the substrate Kneller and Randolph had devised: not only was it harmless to humans, so that it could be eaten by the spoonful and indeed enjoyed because it tasted vaguely savoury, but it required no attention apart from being kept warm and occasionally stirred to let oxygen penetrate to the red veins of pure VC concentrate. Instead of having to be chemically purified, the latter could now simply be removed with a regular hypodermic syringe.

"There's nothing fantastic about it," Malcolm countered. "As you should know by this time."

"Yes, I do, but . . ." Sawyer bit his lip. "The point stands. I'm no chemist. I have sopped up what acquaintances in the forensic department told me, but that apart I'd have said I didn't possess the background to understand the lecture I had from Wilfred and Arthur. Oh, they drilled me through elementary biology and chemistry at school, but I always got low marks, and the data didn't grow into any sort of pattern in my head. Now I understand why VC is what it is, what natural laws govern its behaviour, what effect it has when it enters a living system . . . I can't claim that I took it all in at once. But I certainly didn't need more than about an hour to get the drift, after I'd had the chance to review what had been said."

He shivered. "It's almost as though . . . No, I'll correct that.

It *is* the first time that any creature subject to evolution has been aware that it was happening in present time."

"Yes. I'm sure that's so." Malcolm exchanged one jar for another from the shelf in his kitchenette. "In fact I must have sensed that, I think, when I compared it to loss of the power to excrete allantoin. And what's most significant is the fact that if VC had evolved naturally it would instantly have caught on."

"Didn't someone argue that DDT probably occurred in the course of evolution?" Sawyer said.

"Yes, I've seen mention of that idea." As a loud creak came from overhead, Malcolm winced. "Oh, dear! I used to think it was Billy's weight that made that floor squeal as he walked across it. Ruth's not more than *half* his weight! The central heating must have loosened the nails during the time I could afford to run it." He hesitated a moment. "Hmm! I *can* afford to run it again. I wonder whether I should."

And switched the subject back again. "Yes, if DDT did occur in a natural species, it very likely killed it off!"

"Malcolm, could I ask . . . ? Well, you know I resigned, so I'm out of work, and I'm blacklisted at the Home Office, so I can't set up my own agency or join a security force—which I don't want to do, but couldn't even if I did—and I have a wife and kid, so I wondered if you could . . . Well, you're out of work too, and you've lost your lodgers, all of them, and you're surviving. How?"

"No loss, those lodgers, barring Billy," Malcolm said, and for a moment his face darkened. "Bastards! How I'd like to get even with the godheads who set fire to that club! But . . . Well, last Saturday the weather was good enough for there to be football the first time in two months, right?"

"Yes, I remember."

"So I sent in a pools coupon. I didn't win the jackpot, but I did get twelve thousand pounds. Gambling, I suspect, is among the things that VC will wipe out."

Sawyer's jaw dropped.

"Want a thousand of it?" Malcolm added. "You're welcome.

I can name companies whose shares will double because of
the approaching war. Companies that Charkall-Phelps and
Lady Washgrave have holdings in!"

"That didn't occur to me," Sawyer said. "And it should have
done."

"Why? If the same things occurred to everybody as a result of taking VC, there'd be substance in Ruth's charge about
it turning us into ants. I don't believe there's the least risk of
that happening. The human genetic pool is inconceivably large.
So far, all VC has done is accentuate a bias already there—
provided it was a social bias. Antisocial responses seem to be
overlaid with an enhanced awareness of what it would feel
like to suffer the consequences of the actions that stem from
them. The more I think about this, the more I'm convinced that
we are witnessing an evolutionary advance, neither planned
for by a deity nor the result of blind chance, but a necessary
and highly probable occurrence. Put sufficient quantities of raw
elements a certain distance from a certain type of sun, and
life cannot help but appear. Perhaps if you put a sufficiently
large number of conscious beings in a sufficiently terrible pre-
dicament that may lead to their extermination, they will neces-
sarily hit on the solution to their problems. If that's true, then
we have some very interesting contacts to look forward to in
a century or two, when we've cleaned house."

"I—uh—I get the feeling you mean *we*," Sawyer said after
a pause.

"I very well may," Malcolm conceded. "I don't know about
you, but I've already started to avoid, automatically, some of
the things which I know can accelerate the natural aging of
my body. Later, when we have time and leisure for intro-
spection, I see no reason why we shouldn't analyse the
causes of senility and take very effective steps to postpone
them. We aren't built for immortality, and that's scarcely surprising, but despite our inheritance of a universe in constant
flux there's no obvious reason why we should not attune ourselves to something more like a galactic time-scale."

He hesitated, gazing into nowhere. "Not the present genera-

tion," he said, "but the next after that, ought to be a very remarkable group of people . . . That is, if we can bring them
into existence." He briskened. "And we have that problem in
mind, don't we? And its solution!"

He opened a drawer and produced a hypodermic which he
carefully rinsed before inserting it into one of the widest red
veins in a jar of VC.

"Speaking of godheads, as we were a moment ago," Sawyer
said, "I gather you've had no more trouble with them since
poor Billy died."

"Almost none. It's conceivable that godheads from around
here fired the club, isn't it? Possibly followed him from home.
If so, maybe they feel they've overstepped the mark at last."
Malcolm's tone was stern. "They do still show up one or two
evenings a week, but they've been content to stand begging
in the street rather than invade people's homes. I hope I can
ignore them for the time being."

He closed his eyes for a second. "Matter of fact, they're
about due. If they do come by tonight, it'll be soon."

"You—ah—you're not wearing a watch," Sawyer said.

"Nor are you," Malcolm grunted, transferring the contents of
his syringe into a small jar already primed with the substrate.
"Nor would Ruth be, except that I gave her the one she wears
as a present after the first time we made love."

"I know." Sawyer licked his lips. "Funny, isn't it? I've been
wondering whether the ability to agree on a common sub-
jective time, rather than obey the dictates of clocks, which
are after all machines, may not give us back some of our lost
sense of shared humanity."

"That's a very good point," Malcolm said. He handed over
the jar of VC-infected substrate. "There you are. Harry knows
what to do with it, does he?"

"Oh, yes. And, given what the Australian government has
been saying, that may make all the difference. Their pompous
posturing has made me *sick!* All those hot-air speeches about
how the British have ruined their precious heritage and let
their traditions be eroded by admitting dark-skinned immi-

grants . . . Lord, it's the same process which made English the most flexible and versatile language on the planet."

"And I suspect the only one which can adapt to express what VC endows us with," Malcolm said. "You saw the note that Maurice left."

"Yes, and given that he'd reached a stage even more advanced than you have I see what you mean." Sawyer was hiding the little jar safely in an inside pocket. "Funny!" he muttered. "To think I'm aiding a thief to skip the country . . . Well, circumstances alter cases."

He glanced up alertly, like a dog catching a scent. "By the way, your local godheads appear to have changed their minds, don't they? They've started banging at doors again."

Malcolm concentrated for an instant. "So they have. I wonder why. After the fiery cross was found in the ruins of the Universal Joint, even around here they were being howled down, for the first time ever."

"Perhaps they've taken fresh heart from the fact that Lady Washgrave's Crusade is still packing in the customers. You saw? Eight thousand in Doncaster, eleven thousand in Liverpool . . ."

"How people delude themselves,"' Malcolm muttered. "Sooner or later all the finest ideals of mankind have led to overreaction. Christianity became the official religion of the Roman Empire and was perverted into a justification for slavery. The proud slogan of the French Revolution was inscribed over the guillotine. The oppressed victims of the tsars proceeded to treat their former rulers with even greater brutality."

"It's a fearful pattern," Sawyer sighed.

"But one which we're in a fair way to breaking," Malcolm said. He was absently listening to the oncoming godheads. They were chanting now, sure sign of a large gang of them.

Before Sawyer could comment, Ruth came rushing down the stairs and ran into the room. Daringly, she had put on a pair of tight jeans such as she might have worn ten years ago for the dusty job of clearing out Billy's room and packing up his belongings for return to his parents in America; Lady Washgrave had declared it disgusting for a woman to wear man's clothing, and jeans, pants-suits, slacks, hot-pants, had all vanished from London's streets under a hail of insults and sometimes missiles from her followers.

"Ruth, you look *fantastic!*" Sawyer said. "It must be—oh, two years at least since I saw a woman in trousers, and doesn't it *suit* you?"

She smiled acknowledgement of the compliment, but didn't answer. Instead, she addressed Malcolm.

"Mal, there are godheads on the way—haven't you heard them?"

"Yes, of course we have. So?"

"They must have made a killing today. They're drunk. I have the window open upstairs to blow the dust out, and I can smell whisky on the wind. And glass is being broken, too."

Sawyer, instantly tense, said, "Not windows."

"No, empty bottles, I think."

Malcolm pondered a second. Then he said, "David, how long are you still officially Chief Inspector Jarman-Sawyer?"

"Why, until my four weeks . . . I'm with you. Yes, it will be a pure pleasure."

Ruth glanced from one to the other of them in amazement. "What was all that about—? No, don't tell me. I get it, too. Oh, Mal, I could kick myself, you know, for being so silly when I first realised you'd given me VC! I never had a better present in my life, and I never got one by a nicer means!"

She stretched on tiptoe to kiss his cheek.

"It's so wonderful not to be at a loss any more. All the time in my job I used to find myself staring and staring for half an hour at a time at columns of figures or new tax regulations, waiting for them to make sense . . . Now it happens in a flash. You answer, right? I come down the stairs, and David hangs back until they put their necks in the noose. Fine! A sort of—uh—memorial service for Billy!"

She darted out again.

"Has everyone else shown a similarly positive reaction?" Sawyer inquired.

"Oh, yes. Arthur and Wilfred are still successfully duping this man Gifford, whom I hate on the strength of what they've told me. Bob Bradshaw is recovering steadily—you know he's staying with Hector and Anne? Yes? He's had the worst passage of all of us, even worse than me; he had to undergo the process in ignorance, and what's more in a strange city, and what's *more* he had further to fall, as it were. None of the rest of us had to abandon a long-cherished deep-seated faith; we were all disillusioned in some degree, but 'he was firmly convinced he was on the side of righteousness until VC changed his mind. I *do* wish chance had given us a rabid Marxist, for example, as a control study . . . But Hector says he will be okay in another few days."

"And well enough to play his part in this?"

"Oh, yes. By the way, later tonight I'm expecting Valentine Crawford and his girl-friend to drop in. He's going to sow a bit more VC in—ah—crucial places. Here they come!" he interrupted himself, and turned towards the door.

Five seconds, and the doorbell rang. Malcolm gave a wry grin and headed along the hallway.

"This," he faintly heard from Sawyer, "will make a change!"

He opened the door. At once four burly godheads, with a bespectacled girl following, burst into the hallway, their plastic crosses raised head-high. The first of them he didn't recognise; the one who entered second, however, was the same whom Billy had shouldered down the steps on the day VC broke loose.

"Ah!" the latter cried with satisfaction. "Mr Fry as ever was! Shut the door, you!" he added to the girl, and as number four pushed Malcolm out of the way she compliantly did as she was told.

Very clearly they had all been drinking; the harshness of whisky was fierce in Malcolm's sensitised nostrils.

"A while since you tithed to us, isn't it?" the godhead rasped, while Malcolm convincingly pantomimed agitation. "Last time I remember was before that *bugger* Cohen knocked me over!"

He laughed with relish. "And we all know what became of him, don't we? Good riddance, too!"

"Malcolm, what in the world is—?"

That was Ruth, rounding the curve of the stairs, and stopping dead with her hand to her mouth as she came in sight of the godheads.

"Well, I never!" the spokesman said, staring at her. "The Scarlet Woman herself! Like it both ways, do you, then?" He poked Malcolm in the ribs with the butt of his cross. "Well, someone that perverted owes us a lot more than the average run of decent people. Fifty quid, let's say—shall we?"

"*Fifty?*" Malcolm echoed, feigning horror.

"From each of you," the godhead said. And grinned broadly. "Come on, be quick about it! Otherwise . . . Well, you wouldn't want to wake up one morning and find yourself fried in your bed, would you? All melted down together into a big charred *intimate* lump!" He snapped his fingers at Malcolm. "Come on, let's be having you!"

"You're under arrest," said a quiet firm voice, and David Sawyer appeared from the living-room door, while Malcolm in the same moment pushed the girl in glasses away from the door and set his back to it. "I am Detective Chief Inspector Sawyer, and I am charging you with demanding money with menaces. I warn you that anything you—"

"Malcolm, look out!" Ruth shouted. But Malcolm's newly sharpened reflexes were adequate to cope with the wild swing the nearest godhead aimed. He snatched the heavy cross and used its butt to drive the wind out of its owner, and then the ends of the cross-piece to break the grip of the nearer two of the survivors on their own weapons, and by then Sawyer had tripped up and disarmed the remaining man. The girl simply stood there staring in dismay until Malcolm relieved her of her cross, too; then she started crying.

"Use of reasonable force to prevent them evading arrest," Sawyer said didactically. "Score one, as it were. Ruth, kindly dial nine-nine-nine and ask for a Black Maria to take these ruffians away!"

XX

"You! Kneller!"

The voice was as brutal as a blow from a club. Kneller and Randolph, who had been talking together in low tones close to the big window of the former's office—rain-smeared like half-melted gelatine—spun around in unison to face the door.

"Gifford!" Kneller snapped. "What the hell do you mean by marching in here without an invitation?"

"It's *Doctor* Gifford!" the intruder barked, and strode towards them, fists clenched. "Oh, I know damned well you think I'm a stupid son-of-a-bitch with no right to call myself a scientist—I know because I've overheard you!"

He realised abruptly that his hands were doubled over, and with a visible effort unfolded them and thrust them in the side-pockets of his invariable dark-blue blazer.

"Overheard?" Kneller repeated slowly. "Do you mean you've been—uh—bugging us?"

Gifford ignored that. He said, "But I wasn't such a fool as you thought! Oh, you went to considerable lengths, you displayed considerable ingenuity . . . but it's my job to smoke out traitors, and anybody with the wits of a jackass could tell you're both traitors within an hour of meeting you!"

He was on the verge of ranting; tiny drops of spittle flew from his lips.

"What in the world are you talking about?" Randolph said.

"Your theft of VC!" Gifford blasted. "A theft of government property, what's more!"

"What theft—?" Randolph said, but Kneller cut him short.

"I don't know what you mean when you refer to 'government property'! And I warn you, *Doctor* Gifford—since you

insist on the title—that uttering charges of theft at random
could involve you in a suit for slander, which I must confess
would delight me. I should love to hear you explain in a court
of law how you eavesdropped on private conversations, illegally under the Privacy Act of nineteen seventy-six, and
decided to let fly with wild accusations because you heard
yourself described as what you are!"

Planting his knuckles on his desk, he scowled at Gifford.

With intense difficulty the latter kept his answer down to
a similar conversational level. He said, "Government property,
Professor. On my recommendation, Mr Charkall-Phelps this
morning signed an order requisitioning all stocks of VC wherever they may be located . . . under the provisions of the
National Emergency Act, nineteen seventy-eight!" He straight-
ened to his full height with an expression of triumph.

"I'm sure you thought you were being very clever when
you aped Dr Post's example and filched some VC from these
labs. But you made away with so much of it!"

Randolph and Kneller exchanged meaning glances.

"I don't know what use you have in mind for it," Gifford
went on. "But most likely you've been planning to sell it to the
highest bidder. I know what you're like when you're crossed.
I know how desperately you cling to what you think is right-
fully yours, determined to milk it for everything it can yield!
Regardless of what other people's best interests may dictate!"

He glared furiously from one to the other of them. "It's the
plain duty of someone who makes an invention essential to
national defence to assign it to the government! I say again,
the plain duty! Not that you'd know what the word means
without looking it up in the dictionary, would you?" He sniffed
and turned down the corners of his lips.

"I think I know what's happened," Kneller said, his face
reflecting the great light which had just dawned on him.

"What's happened is that you stole at least a test-tubeful
of VC from these labs and imagined that you could muddle
the trail enough to fool me—me, the man with no right to call

himself a scientist!" Gifford breathed heavily. "But I got on to you! I felt that breath of suspicion which people in my profession learn to respond to."

"Your profession?" Kneller said from the side of his mouth, and without awaiting a reply continued to Randolph, "Arthur, the trustees of the Gull-Grant Foundation."

"Yes. Eager to move us off this potentially valuable site."

"And Washgrave Properties."

"Ditto. Eager to buy."

"And—uh—a certain cabinet minister?"

To that Randolph merely nodded. Gifford, infuriated worse than ever because his bombshell seemed to have left them more instead of less at ease, said sharply, "What are you going on about?"

"We just realised why Charkall-Phelps is so eager to shut us down," Kneller said. "And was already before VC gave him the excuse. What use do you have in mind, Dr Gifford, for this site—assuming it's habitable after the radioactivity has died away?"

Gifford blinked rapidly several times. "I don't know what you're talking about," he said at last. "But you know what I'm talking about. You admit you abstracted a quantity of VC in its substrate from these laboratories!"

"I admit nothing of the sort," Kneller said promptly, and Randolph echoed him.

"Very well, we shall have to place you under arrest, and carry out the necessary tests to determine whether you have indeed illegally ingested VC." Gifford shouted at the door; it swung wide, and two stolid-faced men walked in, while two more waited in the corridor.

"Warrant cards!" Kneller said.

They were duly produced; all four were from Special Branch, the department of the Metropolitan Police concerned with political offences and subversion, which alone of all the police forces in Britain has reported direct to cabinet level since its inception, with no intermediaries.

"You could, of course," Gifford hinted, "avoid considerable indignity and discomfort by admitting where you hid the stolen VC . . . ?"

"You," Kneller said in a calm voice, "are completely and literally insane. Don't worry, though. Nowadays treatment for your type of paranoia is—"

He drew back the necessary few inches to avoid a wild punch Gifford had aimed at his jaw, and glancing at Randolph shook his head sorrowfully.

"Really, it's almost a law of nature," he said. "Defectives of this type find their natural home in the service where suspicious temperaments are at a premium— Oh, really, Dr Gifford!" This time evading a kick with perfect aplomb; it would have hurt like hell if it had landed. "I'm sure this is not in accordance with the regulations you operate under, is it?"

"Heaven give me strength!" Gifford hissed.

"Not unless they've been substantially altered," Randolph said. "I was offered a contract at Hell's Kitchen once, you know." He meant the biological-warfare research establishment at Porton Down to which Gifford had formerly been attached. "I recall the wording of the draft clearly, and it said nothing about kicking and beating people who by retroactive decision of the Home Secretary have committed crimes that aren't actually crimes."

"Precisely," Kneller said. "Even if we did remove a quantity of VC for study away from the interference of Gifford's henchmen, as director of this Institute I was quite entitled to do so, the VC being the property of the Institute."

"It isn't your property!" Gifford flared. "It's a national resource! It could make the difference between our being wiped out as a nation, and our dominating the world again!"

"And," Randolph said softly, "between you being fired for gross incompetence and sitting on the right hand of Lord Protector Charkall-Phelps when he enters into his kingdom!"

"Take them away before I kill them!" Gifford shrieked.

Puzzled, but obedient, the Special Branch men closed in.

"Bob, we're back!" called Anne Campbell. "Would you like some tea?"

"Yes, please!" Rising from the sofa in the living-room, laying aside the newspaper which, it seemed, he had been reading at the same time as he was watching an afternoon news-bulletin on TV. And four-year-old Elspeth hurried to say hello to him, three-year-old Fiona in her wake.

—I have to confess that when Hector said he wanted us to put up an international celebrity who'd had a breakdown . . . Well, I should have known better, I suppose. He's invited lame ducks to stay before, and they all turned out to have some good reason for us paying special attention: that poet who dedicated his next book to us, that poor girl whose husband had nearly strangled her . . . And the children do like him so much!

As he entered the kitchen wearing the children like a collar and a wrist-muff respectively, she greeted him cordially.

"I ought to say how much I appreciate your hospitality," he said as he accepted his teacup. "And tell you that I don't propose to trespass on it any longer."

"Oh, it's been no trouble at all," Anne said. And, after a brief hesitation: "You—ah—you're going home?"

With a wry smile, Bradshaw said, "I don't quite feel up to that for a while, to be honest. Since I'm on this side of the Atlantic, I thought I'd wander around Europe for a few weeks first. Go to Italy, perhaps."

"You think it's safe to go there at the moment?" Anne countered. "I mean, this military take-over they've had . . ."

"All the more reason," Bradshaw said.

"I don't quite see why."

"Well, the only other visits I've made to Europe have been on business, you know. To make personal appearances, or to attend movie festivals—that kind of thing. But there are a few places I've always wanted to see. Rome, for instance. Venice. Naples. If I don't go now, there—well, there may not be anything to see next year."

"Do you really believe the crisis is that serious?" Anne whispered, after glancing to make sure that the children had wandered out of the room again. "Hector was asking whether I wanted to emigrate, you know. To Canada or New Zealand."

"I saw an article in the paper I was just reading which says that emigration levels are at an all-time high," Bradshaw said with a nod.

"Do you think . . . ?" Her voice failed her.

"Do *you* think you should?" he countered.

"I—no. I don't see why I have to! Oh, it may be sensible, but . . . It's the kind of giant upheaval in my life that I want to decide about myself, not have imposed on me!"

"I think the vast majority of people would agree with you. Something's very wrong, isn't it, when you get a forced movement of population owing to something other than natural causes, like earthquakes, or floods?"

"Yes, terribly wrong!"

"And it's started already . . ." He gazed past her, unseeing, towards the window; beyond it, there were shrubs whose branches carried the last greyish remnants of the recent snow. And beyond them again, houses where people could be seen going placidly about their normal business.

"Well . . . All hope is not lost," he said, and drained his cup. At the same moment the front doorbell rang, and he rose promptly.

"That'll be for me. I hope you don't mind—I made some phone-calls while you were out, and I've booked a night flight."

"But . . ." Anne had been going to say that he had no luggage for a continental trip; on reflection, it seemed like a very stupid comment, possibly insulting, and anyhow Fiona was eating something she oughtn't to and required instant salvation.

"Was it a problem?" Bradshaw asked as he accepted what the man at the door had held out to him.

"Not in the least." With a crooked grin. "If I can spring a villain from the toughest remand centre in Britain and see him safely away with a wife and four kids, I can pull almost any trick in the book. A forged American passport is nothing compared to what I've done already."

He added a second item to the first. "And here's your—ah—ration," he went on. "Those capsules are identical with the commonest anti-diarrhoea remedy currently on sale here. I gave Harry the same thing. Nothing's more likely to be taken for granted wherever you go."

"Thanks. Anything else?"

"Best wishes."

"Thanks."

"Cis, are you okay?"

She had put her hands to her head and swayed giddily while reading a story-book to Toussaint. Valentine was busy mixing up substrate for VC in precise accordance with the instructions he had received from Kneller via Malcolm, pausing now and then to glance at the TV. A current-affairs programme was on, the usual ragbag mixture, and French troops had been shown mobilising along the Italian border.

—It's going to be a close thing. If the French and Germans have really agreed to issue an ultimatum . . .

After a long moment and with infinite effort she said, "Val, I think I've been awarded the VC like you said I might."

"Oh!" At once he abandoned his task; it wouldn't suffer from the interruption. "Tous' boy, bedtime—sorry! Cissy isn't feeling too well. No fuss, hear?"

And there was none. Amazingly.

—Nor has there been, come to think of it, since Cissy arrived. There's a problem here we shall have to sort out. Cis spent half her childhood raising younger kids; she got the knack by soaking it through her pores. When there are hardly any children, which has got to happen or we'll eat ourselves out of house and home on this planet, will we be able to . . . ? Shit, of course we shall. Just to watch it happening once will be enough for a lifetime. I keep overlooking what VC can do, even though it's happening right inside my head. And hers too, now.

He was shivering a little as he rejoined her, from awe.

"I'm okay, Val honey," she said in a dull voice. "I just wish, though, you weren't going away tomorrow."

"Baby, I have to," he murmured. "It's important."

"Sure, I know. But it's going to be tough without you. I can stand remembering everything I know, but it makes me realise how many things I *don't* know."

He waited.

"Like—like why that buckra devil carved you. I don't get it. Don't see why he wanted to just 'cause you black. Not like the way I felt when we set out to even the score, you with me? Then I felt I got a purpose, a target I could reach. Even that wasn't worth it, though. Because . . . Hell, he probably didn't know why he treated us so bad, did he? We gave him his own back, and what's come out of it is more hate. When we need less!"

She looked up at him with huge beautiful dark eyes full of hurt.

"Val, taking that box of candy to Lady Washgrave—did it do any more good than fixing that goddamned shopkeeper?"

"A whole lot," Valentine said softly. "You saw the news. She's in hospital, in a coma. Same as I was. Same as Malcolm. Same as Dr Post should have been, except he didn't go sleep it off in time. Too high, maybe. Too sure the initial dose he'd already inhaled was cushioning him against—"

"Val!" she cried suddenly, putting her hands to her head again. "Half of me knows what you mean and half of me doesn't, and the half that doesn't is more—more *me!*"

Stroking her crisp hair comfortingly, he said, "Honey, you and a hell of a lot of other people. A hell of a lot. In the end, the whole damned world. I hope it's soon."

XXI

The phone said, "Malcolm?"

"Yes, David?"

"Get out, fast, and preferably out of the country."

"What? Why?"

"Arthur and Wilfred were arrested by Special Branch this afternoon on Gifford's orders."

A score of alternative plans flashed through Malcolm's mind as he looked along his hallway, imagining the quantities of VC breeding in his kitchenette.

"Very well. Valentine has his, you have yours, Bob has his and is probably on his way by now. Ruth speaks German."

"You speak French?"

"Yes. Thank you. I'll miss the house, though, I must say . . . Still, all being well it'll be here when we come back. 'Bye!"

The news was of the joint ultimatum issued by the other signatories to the Treaty of Rome, demanding that Italy resume adherence to it within twenty-one days. So far there had been no response.

Bradshaw woke from an uneasy doze as the train, which had been grunting up the northerly inclines of Italy, slowed to a halt. He was alone in his compartment; it was clear that even though this was normally a popular resort area the whole year round few people felt inclined to risk heading for it now the crisis was intensifying to the point where the possibility of actual fighting was being openly debated.

He slid up the window-blind, to find grey dawn-light beyond. Half-hidden by mist, mountains white with snow loomed in the distance. And, on a twisting road which at this point the railway overlooked . . .

—Troop-carriers! Half-tracks!

A whole convoy of them, reassigned from duties farther south to judge by the olive-drab of their paint, conspicuous against the off-white piles of snow flung aside from the road. But the men they carried were properly clad for winter in the mountains, wearing all-white insulated clothing and with anti-glare goggles loose around their necks.

The train moved on. Beyond the next curve was another line of military vehicles, this time trucks with snow-chains around their tyres, passing through a small village where a man with bright fluorescent batons was directing them which route to take at an intersection. Early-rising locals were staring in amazement as the tinny bell of the church announced the first mass of the day. It was Sunday.

Bradshaw glanced up at the one lightweight travel-bag he had brought with him, containing something far more important than clothes or shoes or money. His thoughts were grim.

—Still . . . A twenty-one day ultimatum is far better than we were hoping for. Do the meteorologists expect the weather to have broken by then? Right now fighting over this kind of terrain would be as bad as the Russian front in winter 1941.

Not that it would be the same kind of fighting.

Abruptly the door from the corridor was flung open and an officer in a greatcoat and an armed private were demanding, "*I sui documenti!*"

He produced his forged passport and leaned back in his seat unconcernedly. While staying with Hector and Anne he had let his beard grow, then trimmed it neatly into a shape he had never worn in any rôle for movies or TV.

"Ah, you're American, Mr Barton," the officer said as he leafed through the passport. His English was impeccable. "What brings you here?"

—I wonder whether acting will disappear in the Age of VC. When everybody can do it perfectly . . . No, of course not.

It will remain a talent, a greater concern for some people than others. But I never dreamed I could outface suspicious officials so easily. He no more recognises me as Bradshaw than did the immigration people at Milan airport.

"A sentimental journey," he said with a shrug. "My mother's family was Italian. Her name was Gramiani, and her father was born in Piedmont. But he died before I was born."

"I see. Where exactly are you going at present?"

"To a little town which has surprised me by suddenly becoming famous. Arcovado."

—No point in lying about that. But what's the betting he will now search me, and my bag?

The reason for its sudden notoriety was simple. It was the ancestral home of Marshal Dalessandro; his family owned large estates in the neighbourhood. Moreover, he was due to come back to it next weekend, assured of a rapturous welcome.

—But well guarded against assassins, no doubt!

The search followed, as predicted. On finding his travelling medicine-kit, the officer inquired what each item was or carefully read the label. For diarrhoea; indigestion; headache; earache; cuts and bruises . . .

It was clear the officer thought him a thorough hypochondriac. However, he replaced everything and shut the case with a shrug.

"Tell me, Mr Barton," he said musingly, "what do you think of—ah—recent developments here in Italy?"

"Oh, I think a foreigner should defer judgement," Bradshaw answered easily. "Though of course if law and order can be restored and the country regain its prosperity, I'll be one of the first to applaud."

"Good. Thank you, and apologies for putting you to all this trouble." The officer returned his passport and then, struck by an abrupt thought, reached past and slid down the window-blind again.

"Take my advice, and leave it that way for another half-hour," he said with a wry smile. "It may enable you to relax a little more during your vacation."

The news was of reinforcements joining the American Sixth Fleet in the Mediterranean, and of the Austrians following the example of the Swiss and issuing preliminary mobilisation notices to twenty thousand reservists.

So far this morning all had been quiet around the perimeter of the embattled strikers' no-go zone. Having made a complete circuit of the area he was responsible for, Lieutenant Cordery returned to his sergeant at the headquarters radio vehicle.

"I saw a tea-van in the next street," he said. "I think you might as well let the men take ten minutes' break by twos. And—ah—you might get someone to collect a cuppa and a roll of some sort for me, would you?"

"Right, sir!" the sergeant said smartly, and after glancing around pointed at two of the nearest of the shivering soldiers. The snow was lasting much longer here than in the south; there had been a fresh fall last night and the air continued to wear its knife-cruel edge. "You two! Ten minutes for chah and wads. There's a tea-wagon in the next street. And bring some rations back for Mr Cordery."

"Here's fifty pence," Cordery said. "That ought to be enough."

"Okay, sir," the man who took it said, and moved off gratefully. He was out of earshot when he said to his companion, "Well, hell. Never thought the day would come when I'd be glad to see a blackie!"

But Valentine Crawford heard him, and wryly countered inside his head as he put on his best Uncle Tom grin and leaned past the wisp of steam escaping from his big urns.

—Never thought I'd be glad to see a buckra soldier with a gun, baby! But it all adds to the day's business, doesn't it?

Aloud, he merely said, "Yes, gents? Tea, buns, sausage-rolls, ham-rolls, cheese sandwiches—all here and waiting!"

"Hah!" one of the soldiers said, looking at the neat piles of food under their scratched plastic domes. "Not doing much trade, are you?"

"Only just started for the day, sir. Thought you ought to have first call!" Broadening his grin still further.

"We deserve it, no doubt of that. Okay, tea, and plenty of sugar. And a cheese sandwich."

"Coming up!"

Over the next week, he became a familiar and popular visitor to the nearby streets.

The news was of Russian forces being unexpectedly assigned to "manoeuvres" in southern Hungary, and a call for stern resolution in the face of trial issued by the Right Honourable Henry Charkall-Phelps at a giant Moral Pollution rally in Birmingham, where he was cheered nonstop for almost five minutes.

—So little of it available . . . If only Malcolm hadn't had to flee, destroying half of what we'd painfully bred for fear Gifford's people might discover traces of it! I'm not sure he had tracked the connection between Malcolm and the Institute, but obviously he must have been monitoring phone-calls from and to there, so the risk was acute.

Sawyer shifted from foot to foot and blew into his hands. It was chilly waiting here in the line for admission to the Public Gallery of the House of Commons, but it seemed like an absolutely perfect target, far better than cinemas or tube-trains or other obvious possibilities. Particularly today, when it was being rumoured that at long last Charkall-Phelps would launch his personal attack on the Prime Minister, expected since his recent veiled insults on TV and at public meetings. Of course, it would not be in the gentlemanly tradition of British politics to hold a fight out in the open; the real business would be conducted behind the scenes, so that the country would eventually be presented with a *fait accompli* under the guise of democratic process. But certain aspects of what was happening might now and then be glimpsed between the drifting smoke-clouds of verbiage.

—Even if I don't manage to get to the head of the line in time for the big speech of the afternoon, it'll be worth going in anyhow. And I've already done marvels, though I say it myself. That special service for forces chaplains at St Paul's yesterday: that was a real stroke of luck! I wonder whether Malcolm's friend at the Epidemic Early Warning Unit has begun to notice another outbreak of this curious variety of narcolepsy . . . Probably not. We're having to spread the VC so thinly, it's an even chance whether people are actually receiving the threshold dose. Apart of course from Lady Washgrave. Reminds me: I should see how Cissy's doing.

The news was of shouting-matches behind closed doors at EEC Headquarters in Brussels, with the big countries' delegates—those from France, West Germany and Britain—insisting on a hard line and the literal execution of the ultimatum, while the smaller countries, led by the Dutch, were claiming that there would be no way of confining a war if it broke out, and although big nations might have a faint hope of surviving nuclear attack small ones would be completely depopulated with half a dozen bombs.

Not that anyone ought to have needed to be told.

This winter, the most popular of all restaurants as a rendezvous for members of the Bonn parliament was *Am Weissen Pferd*, whose proprietor was a great sentimentalist. On noticing an attractive dark-haired woman weeping openly before one of the city's countless monuments to Beethoven, it was only natural that he should stop and inquire what was the matter.

Having been reassured that she was in tears purely because she was overwhelmed by the awareness of walking on ground Beethoven himself had trodden, he equally naturally invited her to visit his restaurant. He was married and had three grown children, but he was a notorious womaniser.

Besides, he was extremely proud of his cuisine, and took her on a tour of his kitchens to demonstrate that even in this heavily polluted land of Western Germany it was possible to eat at certain places, even now, without risking one's health because the food was contaminated with artificial substances, preservatives or insecticides or flavour-enhancers.

Fascinated, she inquired why he did not offer sea-salt, but had ordinary commercial salt on every table, and he told the sad story of the salt from Aigues-Mortes which had proved to contain more than one per cent of some fearful industrial waste-product, and resulted in many of a rival restaurant's clientèle being taken to hospital.

He had not, as it happened, heard of Maldon salt, from the still relatively uncontaminated North Sea, and by way of making a gesture towards repayment of his hospitality and generosity she obtained some for him, which he had tested and was able with a clear conscience to give his guests. Overjoyed, he asked her advice in other matters, and was equally pleased to discover that she herself was an immensely knowledgeable cook.

—If he only knew that it's all book-learning . . . But VC does make the most incredible acts of imagination possible. Like reading the score of a symphony; Ernest Newman once said that was a purer pleasure than listening to even the best orchestra under the best conductor! A cook-book can be a banquet for me now. Luckily eating is still better, in my view, or I could find myself sitting over a bowl of soup, reading about a gourmet meal, and paying no attention to the muck I was actually ingesting. Didn't realise until now how much of what we're sold as food really is muck. Dangerous, too . . .

When she produced, with a flourish, a seasoning he had never heard of but which at her table at least, in the small apartment she had temporarily rented, seemed to make the simplest food taste exquisite, he had no qualms at all about trying it out at *Am Weissen Pferd*.

Where, sadly, the majority of the customers continued to

do as they had always done: drink so much they blunted their sense of taste, smoke between courses and even during them, and leave half the food on the plate.

But that was politicians for you. And with the clouds gathering over Europe, it was perhaps less than surprising.

The news was of a mounting roar of support in Italy for the New System of Marshal Dalessandro, of recognition of his government by Greece first, then Spain, then Portugal, then the United States. And of air-raid warnings being tested, and shelter-drills for schoolchildren, and the printing of ration-cards.

"Que je suis désolée, mais aujourd'hui il n'est pas vraiment possible!" the madam exclaimed, and it was obvious that she really meant it. Within a week or so of his arrival this English milord—unmistakably a milord, even though he was travelling incognito as a plain *mee-stair*—had become the most popular client her house had ever had. "It is the *armée*," she added by way of explanation, and spread her hands.

"Mais je comprends parfaitement," the Englishman said. And did. The existence of this streetful of brothels in this small garrison town was tolerated on conditions, chief among which was that when one of the locally stationed regiments was dispatched for active service its men would have first call. "Another time, then. For tonight, perhaps you would distribute these among the girls as a token of my appreciation?"

He snapped his fingers, and the young man who seemed to be his valet produced an armful of expensive and delicious candy, at least a dozen boxes.

Receiving them with cries of exaggerated gratitude, the madam whispered, "Milord—I mean *monsieur*—it is not only you who are appreciative. I swear, never have I seen before such a phenomenon as yesterday, when a girl came to me who I *know* never touched a man in her life except in the course of the profession, who has always saved her heart for other women. And said if there is a man who might change her, it would be you. Milord, it is of the most extraordinary!"

—Madam, you ain't seen nothing yet. Promise, promise.

"*A bientôt, madam,*" he said, turning away.

"*Oui, Monsieur Fraïl A bientôt!*"

XXII

"Oh, milady, you're awake at last," cried Tarquin Drew, and in his excitement almost dropped the flowers he had brought to replace yesterday's, now drooping on the bedside table in this neat clean hospital room.

"I woke up hours ago," Lady Washgrave snapped, laying aside the *Daily Telegraph* she had been reading. "They tried to telephone you, apparently, but you didn't answer!"

Tarquin blushed brilliant crimson.

"I—uh . . . Well, for some reason, milady, I've been oversleeping. Even though I've been retiring early for the past three days, I've slept until nearly ten A.M. each morning." He essayed a little joke. "Sympathetic magic, perhaps!"

He sat down eagerly at the side of the bed, and then caught sight of the headlines on the *Telegraph*. "Oh, you must know already the great news I was going to impart!" he exclaimed. "What a shame!"

"What 'great news'?"

"Why, that Mr Charkall-Phelps is almost certain to oust the Prime Minister at the next meeting of the Parliamentary Party!"

"It'll be a sad lookout for the country if he does," Lady Washgrave grunted.

"Why, milady! What on earth makes you say—?"

"What he's been saying makes me say!" she interrupted. "Since I woke up I've had a chance to catch up on these speeches he's been making. The man's mad. Should have realised it years ago."

Totally disoriented, Tarquin could only stare.

"*Must* be mad!" she declared. "The way he's talking, you'd think he was a reincarnation of Churchill and the enemy were lining up to invade! Going on about our determination to withstand the most appalling onslaught, confident in our great traditions, and the rest of it. I'd like to see him try and stop an H-bomb with fine words and flowery phrases!"

She glared at him. "Oh, he fooled me all right, I have to admit that. It's only now he's coming into the open, showing himself up for what he is—a thoroughgoing megalomaniac!"

"But, milady—!"

"It's perfectly clear," she snapped. "Perfectly clear, at long last. If I'd been at the last few rallies of the Crusade, I'd have given him a piece of my mind! Hah! I take back everything I said about Brother Bradshaw. He saw through the sham at once, and I should have done, and I didn't. To my lasting disgrace! I knew perfectly well that if he was a business associate of George's he must be a bad egg, and I hid the truth from myself."

"I—I honestly don't follow you," Tarquin whimpered.

"Well, you never knew George. And even if you had met him you might not have caught on. You're easily fooled by charm, aren't you?" And, as he bridled, she gave a harsh laugh. "Oh, you know perfectly well you are! Maybe because you have so much of it yourself. Even more than George. Of course, I don't suspect you of hiding anything under it half as bad as what he did. Vicious bastard."

"Milady, I—!" Tarquin seemed on the verge of crying.

"Brace yourself, man! You know damned well this is a hell of a world we live in, and lying here I've realised that the effort *I've* put into trying to make it better was like—like wallpapering a room to hide the cracks and the dry rot! I even managed it inside my own head. But"—her expression changed suddenly; she looked inexpressibly miserable—"but I can't fool myself any more, Tarquin. It hurts dreadfully, but I have to put an end to it. I have to admit that I knew without knowing how George made that fantastic fortune of his."

There was a dead pause. Eventually Tarquin said, "In—ah —property, surely!"

"By driving people out of their homes, Tarquin! I was living with him. I knew, all right! I just pretended to myself that I didn't. That's one of the reasons I was glad when he dropped dead."

"Glad?" he echoed in horror. And then, with an unexpected access of boldness, "Milady, can I say something? I"—he had to swallow—"I can't help wondering whether when you called him vicious just now, you meant . . ."

It broke off there.

"Vicious to me?" Lady Washgrave said. "Oh, yes. True to type in marriage and out. And I don't mind who knows it. Not now. There's a word I've often read but never until now grasped the true meaning of: *catharsis*. Like having a boil lanced in your soul. I've been hiding knowledge of something foul from myself, under a veneer of 'good works'. I hope I never delude myself that way again."

"But your work has been good!" Tarquin insisted. "You've done marvels!"

"Good enough to repay the people who were driven out of their homes to make the fortune I enjoy?" rasped Lady Washgrave. "And you of all people should condemn some of the consequences I've aided and abetted, like what led to that gay club being burned out and seven people killed!"

Tarquin gasped. "Milady, I—"

"Come off it, you're as queer as a coot and you know it and I know it and to be absolutely honest the only thing I can genuinely regret about it is that it means I can't invite you into bed with me. George was the only man I ever had, and he was so unspeakably incompetent I don't suppose our marriage ever recovered from the ghastly honeymoon he inflicted on me. Of course I took it for granted that that was how all men behaved to their wives, but it obviously can't be true because so many women actually *like* sex." She eyed him speculatively. "It may be a bit late in my life but I do feel it's high time I—Tarquin!"

But he had rolled his eyes upward in their sockets and slid off his chair in a dead faint.

It was forty-nine hours before he reawakened.

The news was of frantic in-front-of-the-scenes speeches declaring determination to stand firm and not to compromise and frantic behind-the-scenes negotiations undertaken in the intervals of trying to find the right person to bribe for a booking on a ship or plane bound for the Southern Hemisphere and drafting advertisements to sell desirable residential properties at ridiculously low prices, "owner unexpectedly posted overseas".

But there was reference, a long way down the News in Brief column, to a curious sickness afflicting troops on duty in Glasgow.

"Well, Vee, how d'you like Canberra?" Harry Bott said proudly.

"Don't," she answered sullenly. "Not much, anyway."

"Ah, I know it's going to be tough for a while. But I have a job already, don't I? Not much of a job, but enough to make ends meet. With one of the best air-conditioning companies in the whole of Australia!"

"And all of us packed in two rooms!" she snapped back. "At least at home we'd have been in four rooms!"

"If we'd stayed at home I'd be in jail!" Harry exploded.

"Yes, and it'd have been no loss . . ." Vera pushed back a stray tress of hair from her face. It was beginning to grey near the roots.

And then, as if she had overheard herself say that in memory, "Harry! I didn't really mean it! Don't hit me!" She cringed away from him, one arm raised as though to ward off a blow.

—Lord. Have I made her that scared of me? I suppose I must have. Makes me so angry with myself, deep inside. I feel ashamed. There's more to life than playing out a part. I been doing that far too long.

He reached for the bottle of Foster's beer which he had going and hesitated as he poised it over his glass. "Er—want some?" he ventured. "You haven't tasted this Aussie beer yet, have you?"

Not quite believing that he hadn't hit her, she lowered her arm slowly and stared at him.

"Harry, what's come over you?" she said at last.

"I'll tell you one day," he grunted. "For the time being mark it down to my being so pleased that I'm here, not sweating out five years' bird!"

—And . . . Well, I don't know how he fixed it, I really don't. But I'm going to keep my side of the bargain I made with Mr Sawyer. When those new air-conditioning units go into that posh hotel all the MP's and diplomats use, there's going to be that little gadget added to each one I can get my hands on. Not much to pay back for years of extra life, is it?

"I'll find you a glass," he said. "Or a cup, or something."

The news was of a crisis in Japan, with a fervent right-wing movement demanding that advantage be taken of the mess Europe was drifting into, and of a violent argument between those Australian politicians who maintained that old loyalties required them to support the British government come what may, and their opponents, who declared that the British had long ago cut them loose by their repeated perfidy.

And the days of the ultimatum were wearing down, like rock eroded by the swift tumult of a river.

"Oh, it is a very great day for all of us here in Arcovado," the priest said, rubbing his hands as he led Bradshaw through the bitterly cold church. In the past week he and his American visitor had become fast friends. Belying his modest disclaimers about his ignorance of the language, the latter had been able to pose amazingly technical questions about ritual, vestments, the sacrament of the mass, and other abstruse theological subjects, and had shown a greater and greater interest in the Roman confession, to the point where the priest was if not confident at least optimistic about the chance of welcoming this declared heretic into the fold.

"Yes!" he went on. "Without misusing the term, one might well refer to Marshal Dalessandro as the saviour of Italy, the man who will restore the true faith . . . Forgive me, I am admittedly prejudiced in that area!" He laughed as he opened the door from the nave into the little stone-walled room where the raw materials, as it were, lay waiting: the wafers and the wine, not yet transubstantiated by blessing.

"To think that in the morning he and so many of the famous will take the communion here! Oh, it's the fulfilment of a dream, the answer to a thousand prayers . . . Excuse me, is something wrong?"

Bradshaw was sniffing the air suspiciously.

"Father, you'll forgive me if I mention a most delicate subject, I'm sure," he said. "Perhaps through long habit you simply do not notice, but . . . Ah—is there sewage somewhere nearby?"

The priest blinked rapidly several times. The point sank home. He said, "Oh!"

"I believe I'm right," Bradshaw said. "There is an open drain to windward of here somewhere. While I'm certain that in cold weather it can lead to no possible harm, the aroma, the effluvium . . . Your distinguished visitors, after all, do hail from somewhat more prosperous localities!"

"Yes, how terrible, I should have thought of it before, with so little time to go before the great occasion . . . !" The priest was close to babbling in his agitation.

"Never mind, leave it to me," Bradshaw said.

"You, Mr Barton? You can help me?"

"I can indeed. By pure chance I happen to have with me one of the newest aerosol products from America. It will disguise unpleasant stinks more efficiently than the finest of all possible incense. Allow me to offer it to you in the morning prior to the mass which Marshal Dalessandro will attend."

"And two other cabinet ministers, and the commander-in-chief of the armed forces, and hundreds of journalists, and—oh, the Good Lord knows who else!" Clasping his hands, the priest turned to Barton-Bradshaw.

"What requires to be done?"

"Merely that I should come here a little early, perhaps by half an hour, and wander around spraying it in the most strategic places. That is all."

"I shall make sure you are admitted," the priest promised,

and could not restrain himself from embracing the marvellously helpful stranger. "What a shame, Signor Barton, that you are not of our persuasion, for clearly you have its interests at heart, and what is more those of the country from which your ancestors hailed!"

"But of course," Bradshaw said modestly. "Would a man be able to call himself a man if he did not?"

—If the officer who searched my bag on the train were to learn of this and start wondering how I laid hands on this "new aerosol from America", there'd be trouble. Thank goodness (a very interesting phrase, indicative of the way human thinking may well develop in the next age after ours, invoking pure concepts rather than hypothesising personal deities . . . but skip that!) it takes VC to make one treat that kind of insight as a matter of course. I'm half-scared by the success of this plan. One could not be *sure* until his helicopter landed that Dalessandro was going to do the "obvious thing" and celebrate his birthday in a suitably symbolic fashion, here on the land his ancestors used to farm. One makes a guess: human beings react more predictably the more stress they have to endure. Small wonder, if so, that governments have always found it easier to cope with a population threatened by war, unemployment, epidemic, injustice, what have you? A totally free man is also totally unpredictable to anyone else who is not himself free. And in Donald Michael's immortal phrase, "anyone who offers himself for election under a democratic system automatically disqualifies himself, because those who crave power are those least fitted to wield it!" Addicts. That's what they are.

"Why do you smile, Signor Barton?" the priest inquired.

"Because I'm pleased to do you this small service," Bradshaw returned, bowing. "You, and everybody!"

The news was of a form of narcolepsy.

It seemed to have no aftereffects worth mentioning. It certainly did not adversely affect the health of any known patient. And it did not appear to be an epidemic in the formal sense.

There was no clear vector-pattern, as far as computer studies could reveal.

It was fairly common in Glasgow.

There was a discernible incidence in London and elsewhere in the Southern Counties of England.

There were foci in Bonn and in the South of France, not far from the Italian border.

There were minor outbreaks in and around Rome, connected in a manner which did hint at the possibility of a link with other affected areas, inasmuch as everyone concerned had been at the same place at the same time.

But on the other hand there was a totally separate outbreak in Australia, and it was suggested by authoritative experts that the likeliest common cause was stress. The persons who succumbed were typically involved in politics or some other extremely demanding occupation, such as active service with the forces, or else were facing a crisis of conscience of unparalleled severity. The spokesmen cited army chaplains in particular, who were confronted with the dilemma posed by the risk of nuclear war, and those soldiers who had been day and night on patrol in the riot areas of Glasgow.

Meantime, Down Under, there was the traumatic experience in progress of taking for the first time in Australian history a genuinely independent policy decision without reference to an overriding loyalty.

Not that, in fact, a great deal of attention was paid to this minor mystery. There was too much else to worry about: above all, the warning just issued by the Soviet Union that the United States was to treat the dissension in the Common Market as a purely internal matter, or must face the consequences of meddling in it.

The world was singing a note of hysteria now, like the string of a violin tightened to the limit of its strength.

XXIII

"*Voici le journal, m'sieur*," the chambermaid said, and added as she set down the paper and a tray with his morning coffee at Malcolm's bedside, "*Quelque chose d'incroyable vient d'arriver à Londres, paraît-il!*"

Malcolm sat up frantically and seized the paper, giving only a glance at the window beyond which the grey morning light typical of Brussels showed him roofs dripping moisture like leafless boughs in a lonely forest . . . though with no expectation of turning green upon the advent of spring. It had taken a while to work out why he found this city the most depressing of any he had ever visited, barring the dismal towns of the industrial north of England. He had deduced at last that what it lacked was water. A river, or even a canal, would have given it shape and some extra dimension the human psyche needed on a deep obscure level.

But this was no time for reflection. The headlines stated that the new British Prime Minister, M. Charkall, was . . .

He stared, not believing his eyes, and then began to laugh. And laughed, and laughed, so loudly and so long that the girl who had delivered his tray came back to inquire anxiously what was wrong.

"Oh, bless you, David!" he forced out at last. "Helping the police with their inquiries into offences under the . . . No, it's too much!"

—Has there ever been a case like this before? There have been MP's who ran afoul of the law, like Horatio Bottomley, and others who were screwed by a scandal, from Profumo to Parnell. But a Prime Minister . . . ! How? How?

He was scanning the story as fast as he could. It was continued on page two. Turning, he discovered the key to the puzzle.

"Amelia," he said softly. "So it worked even on a case-hardened old figurehead like her."

What had happened was not spelled out in the paper. It was all plain to him, though. Lady Washgrave had suffered a fit of conscience on realising with intolerable clarity where the fortune she had inherited had stemmed from. And she had gone to the Director of Public Prosecutions.

And prior to his entry into politics, ten years ago, one of the directors of Washgrave Properties had been Henry Charkall-Phelps.

And very likely thanks to David Sawyer, the PM had not been able to hide the fact that he had connived at the kind of unsavoury—

Another paragraph elsewhere on the page caught his eye, and his train of thought broke off, derailed.

—Troops deserting in Glasgow? *Fourteen* courts-martial? Oh, it's all happening, it's really all happening! But how about the bloody French? Surely by now something ought to— But there it is! On page three!

He read hungrily, scarcely daring to credit the agency the dispatch was from. Reassignment of the 18th Infantry Division . . . resignation of a senior officer . . . political differences in the ranks leading to . . .

Aloud he told the air, "If I'd written my own script, I couldn't have improved on *this*."

"So what do you think will happen?" Sawyer asked the barman who was drawing his mid-morning pint.

"Dunno," the man grunted. "Except one thing. *I* know we've been led by fools and rogues, but this is the first time we've ever been led by a *criminal!*"

With a snort he turned to serve someone else. Sawyer smiled quietly into his beer.

"*Ach, Liebchen,* it is beyond belief!" sighed the owner of *Am Weissen Pferd*. "Last night, it was a calamity! Nobody ate anything—anything at all bar a token mouthful! There was the most terrible scene in front of all the other customers, when this member of the *Bundestag* shouted across the room at Herr General Kleindienst, calling him a crazy killer who wanted to play with atom-bombs like children's toys, to sit safely in a concrete bunker and watch the pretty flames as they exploded!"

"But it's true, isn't it?" Ruth murmured, stirring her coffee.

"True? But of course not! It is necessary that we have these weapons to save us from the Russians, who would otherwise walk in and steal our land from us! Not that someone with a memory as long as mine could *entirely* hold that against them, for I myself . . ."

Patiently she endured for the umpteenth time the recital of his experiences on the Russian front in World War II, and noted with interest that today, unprecedentedly, he interspersed accounts of his own heroism with references to the plight of the peasants whose land the great battles had been fought over.

—It's working. I wish I knew where Malcolm was! I'd so love to phone him and share this triumph.

"Morning, Val," said the sergeant in a dispirited tone. He and Valentine had become quite well acquainted now. "The usual, please . . . No, make it a sausage-roll today. I feel like a change."

"Coming up, sarge!" Valentine said, turning to his urns. And unable to resist glancing at the sugar he had so carefully doctored every evening in his squalid lodgings since he arrived. Once you had the knack of growing VC, it was no more difficult than, say, making cottage cheese. Though it did provoke raised eyebrows when he bought the ingredients for the substrate.

"You been having trouble, sarge?" he added in a sympathetic tone.

"Trouble? Trouble is putting it mildly!" The sergeant took a moody bite of his roll. "Losing Lieutenant Cordery that

13

way—never saw nothing like it in my life. You know what he did?"

"Well, I heard *something* . . ."

"Probably didn't hear the half! Called us all together and started giving us this lecture on how if the government had worked everything out properly to start with, there wouldn't be any strikers throwing bombs and sniping at us, and then the colonel interrupted and had him put under arrest, and . . . But tell me something, Val. How do *you* feel?"

Valentine hesitated only fractionally. He put on a disapproving tone.

"Sarge, I was brought up to think that this was a good country, a great country. Even if they did drag my grandfather off to be a lousy slave, they realised it was wrong, they passed laws, they gave us something to make up. And to be here now and see what's damned near civil war—well!" He handed over the plastic cup with four spoonfuls of sugar, which he knew this customer liked.

"Right. *I* didn't sign on to shoot at jocks," the sergeant said. "Nor at micks. Hell, I've served with both, and there's some good and some bad in them all, same as with English people. I've had my bellyful. And, what's more"—with growing decision—"I'm going to go tell that bugger of a captain! Just as soon as I finish this tea. You make bloody good teà, you know."

Valentine shrugged and spread his hands.

"No, I mean it! Funny, but I only just got to thinking about it. Good food. Best fish and chips I ever ate came from a shop run by a bod from Cyprus. Near where I used to live. That was all you could do for a meal late on Saturday after the pubs shut, until a Chinese restaurant opened up, and then an Indian one just around the corner, too. Good scoff, most of it. Bit weird for the likes of me to start with, but— No, I was forgetting. You were born here, Val, right? I mean in London, same as me!"

He gulped the last of his tea and replaced his empty cup on the counter of the van. "Thanks! Now I *am* going to give 'em a piece of my mind!"

Very cautiously the adjudant moved aside the branches of
the bush at the crest of the hill, still so tightly wrapped in
frozen snow that he could hear them crackle, and raised his
binoculars to look towards Italy.

And uttered a gasp that must have been audible for half
a mile.

Of all the spectacles that could be presented to an officer
commanding troops there was none, in his opinion, more
ghastly than the sight that now met his eyes.

Down there, scarcely a hundred metres off, were the members of the patrol he had sent out at dawn, and who had been
missing since an hour later. He had signalled the *Quartier-
Général* about them. Now, more than likely, indignant notes
would be flying back and forth between Paris and Rome—by
way of Geneva, since of course the French government had
broken off diplomatic relations with the Italians after their
appalling treachery—and they were not dead at all!

They were here in plain sight, sitting around and chatting
and exchanging cigarettes and gulps of wine with their Italian
enemies-to-be!

Careless of consequences, he rose into plain sight and approached them at a crunching run, drawing his automatic.

"Are you mad?" he screamed at the corporal leading the
patrol.

The latter looked at him coolly, and answered in a lazy
drawling voice.

"Why, no, *mon adjudant*. Rather, we have come to our
senses. We have been thinking, you know. We have been
wondering why, if our leaders are so eager for us to die on
their behalf, they couldn't have given us something first. I
speak little Italian, but enough to discover that this poor
bougre"—pointing at one of the nearer *bersaglieri,* in white
except for the dark panes of his snow-goggles—"is a Catholic
like myself, and has three children, like myself, and had to join
the army because he could not find another job that would pay
to support his family. Like myself."

He calmly took a swig of wine; the bottle being passed con-
tained, according to its label, Valpolicella.

"Want some?" he added. "It's not bad. Not good, because it's so cold, but not bad."

"You're under arrest!" the *adjudant* barked. He raised his gun. Instantly, twenty other guns were levelled at him, both French and Italian . . . although in fact they were all made in Belgium. Identical.

"Mon adjudant," the corporal said, "we have been talking for about an hour. Despite our lack of interpreters, we have made better progress in that hour than the United Nations can make in a year! We are agreed that before we kill each other we should better serve mankind by killing those who order us to kill each other. Why do you not behave sensibly and sit down and discuss your views with us? We had just touched on something that I myself detest about the army life: the way we soldiers are given the chance of contact with a woman as a kind of supplement to our pay, whereas it is the natural right of us all. I do not deny that I have myself taken advantage of such offers, and indeed did so the night before we were sent here. But in principle I think it is not right, because such a commercial transaction . . . Ah, forgive me. You would not of course have indulged, would you?"

The *adjudant,* with a cry of rage, aimed his pistol. A shot rang out. The pistol vanished from his hand like a conjuring trick and flew into a bank of snow.

"I hope that did not hurt so very much," the Italian who had fired said in broken French with a terrible accent. "Is better, though, not? Please, sir, have cheese, a cigarette, something! Is better French cheese yes, we agree, but is better Italian cigarettes, we think. Each have something proudly of . . . Ah, hm, uh?" He appealed with his eyes for assistance, bogged down in the morass of translation.

But the *adjudant* had turned and fled. Behind him he heard laughter.

And jokes about his inability to satisfy a woman.

"Tell me something, Professor," said the lawyer Kneller had engaged to represent himself and Randolph.

"Yes?"

"Have you ever studied law?"

"No, never."

"Then how on earth did you manage to give me the best layman's brief I've ever received? I never saw anything clearer or more detailed in all my—what is it now?—twenty-eight years of practice!"

Kneller gazed modestly at the floor. "Well, one of my best friends at Oxford was reading law, and I do number quite a few solicitors and barristers among my personal acquaintances."

The lawyer snorted. "Then all I can say is that you've missed your vocation. You have a rare aptitude for legal argument." He was turning the pages of the brief as he spoke. "Beautifully organised—beautifully! And there isn't a hole anywhere!"

"That's very kind of you. But the important question is: will it do its job?"

"You mean will it get you and Dr Randolph out from under these absurd charges? Of course it will—not a shadow of a doubt." The lawyer hesitated. "As a matter of fact I believe the charges would be set aside anyway, but it's always more satisfying, so to speak, to know you had a winning hand despite your opponent throwing in his cards. You are aware that one of the most extraordinary cases in the whole of English jurisprudence is just about to break?"

"I take it you're referring to the remarkable coincidence in time between the selection of Charkall-Phelps as the new PM, and his investigation by the police for various rather unsavoury offences connived at, if not committed, during his time as a director of Washgrave Properties?"

The lawyer threw up his hands. "God's name! If half the charges are true, he should have spent the past ten years in jail, not in the House of Commons!"

"As a matter of purely clinical interest," Kneller said, "they are *all* true. But if you don't mind my changing the subject—how soon are you going to get me out of here?"

"Oh, within a few minutes. Just as soon as Chief Superintendent Gladwin arrives. You heard he's taken over from Owsley?"

"I hadn't heard, in fact, but I'm not surprised. Is Owsley going to face disciplinary action?"

Staring, the lawyer said, "For a man who's been under arrest since before this affair came into the open, you're astonishingly well informed. Yes, it seems likely, and among the things he's going to have to answer for I'll make sure they include unreasonable opposition to bail for you and Dr Randolph."

"You might also drop a hint in the right quarter," Kneller said, "about his inability to solve the murder of my late colleague Dr Post, which in fact was solved by the man he displaced from the investigation, David Sawyer, and—"

"And who was so affronted by this high-handed treatment that he felt obliged to resign," the lawyer supplied. "I heard about that, and I was shocked. Obviously Sawyer was a dedicated and gifted officer; wasn't he also responsible for arresting that drug-peddler, Feathers? I imagine I'd have done the same in his place. Oh, I think I can say with certainty that this creeping personality-cult which over the past few years has been infecting the police, since the advent of Charkall-Phelps as Home Secretary, is at an end."

He gathered his papers and rose.

"I'll just go and see whether Gladwin is here yet. If he is, I'll be back at once and you'll be a free man again in a matter of minutes."

On came the floodlights, and the square, packed with workers returned from abroad, waved in their brilliance, like a field of grass when a breeze passes over it on a sunny day. This was where Marshal Dalessandro had drawn his support since the very beginning, in the stock populist tradition. Some of those people waiting for him tonight were former factory-hands in Birmingham, garage-attendants in Munich, night-watchmen in Lyons, dockside roustabouts in Antwerp . . . whose work had vanished thanks to economic forces they could not comprehend, and who had been compelled to come home trailing the dismal shreds of their vision of the Promised Land.

Disappointment had matured into anger. They wanted a messiah at all costs, and in Dalessandro they had found one. Elsewhere and at other times the shirtless ones had turned in similar fashion to Mussolini, to Perón, to Adolf Hitler—and sometimes been gratified, often not.

Now, when the marshal emerged, he looked pale and strained; it was known that he had been for two and a half days victim of this extraordinary sleeping-sickness one had read about. On seeing him recovered, the crowd exploded with delight.

When, after three or four minutes, there was quiet, he approached the waiting microphones . . . and hesitated, looking from one side to the other of the square, with a special smile for the TV cameras. And finally seemed to brace himself, and spoke up: "My friends!"

"*Il nostro Duce!*" came an answering roar.

"My friends!" he repeated. "I have great news for you! It has come to me, as though in a vision, how we can spare our beloved land from the scourge of war!"

There was a near-silence, in which could almost be heard the thoughts of his listeners: "But we were looking forward to that!"

He went on doggedly. "We have the tools in our hands to make a good life for everybody. They have been ignored, they have been neglected. Those who neglected them were perhaps evil, or—more likely—they were unable to cope. Our world is so complicated, and so many decisions have to be taken, and so many people are trying to extract maximum benefit for themselves at the expense of others . . . But today I offer you a plan which will benefit everybody, and nobody will be deprived!"

Half an hour later, those of the reporters who were not clapping as wildly as the crowd were saying to each other, "But why didn't anybody think of that before? It's *obvious!*"

XXIV

"One thing does please me immensely," Malcolm said as he dexterously opened celebratory bottles of champagne in the small, and now crowded, living-room which Maurice Post had formerly rented. He had found on returning to London that in a final wild spasm of blind fury a godhead gang had attacked his house with fire-bombs and burned it to the ground, as though the war which had been so efficiently aborted had needed to leave some warning traces on the world. But that had been virtually the last such incident.

"What, darling?" Ruth inquired, taking the freshly filled glasses and distributing them. It was going to be a grand party, this; perhaps never in all of history had there been so good an excuse for holding one.

"That there's still room for sentiment," Malcolm said.

"I know what you mean," Kneller agreed. "In a sense, the whole thing began here, didn't it? Here in Maurice's home. It must have been here that he first realised he was being affected by VC—here that he debated with himself hour after hour trying to work out whether his views concerning the fate in store for the world were justified, or illusory—here that he took the crucial decision to try it on himself, to be a guinea-pig on behalf of mankind."

"He had guts," Cissy said. She was sitting in a nearby chair with Toussaint perched on her knee. The boy was looking very annoyed. He had insisted on trying the champagne for himself, and concluded it was a confidence trick.

"More guts than most," Valentine said with a nod. "A real hero, that guy." And, having sampled the glass of champagne

Ruth handed to him, interrupted himself to say, "Hey, that's delicious!"

"I was just going to say the same," David Sawyer chimed in. "I never used to take seriously all the fine phrases the experts used about wine. A pint of keg has always been my regular tipple. But since catching VC I've developed quite a palate, and this is a marvellous drink."

"I can see one person who disagrees with you," Ruth murmured dryly. "I'll get Toussaint some apple-juice. Won't be a moment." She vanished in the direction of the kitchen.

"Heroes!" Valentine said, reverting to his former point. "I don't see how they got away with it for so long, giving phony examples to kids—people who like held the bridge, or went on fighting with one arm and one eye. Me, I'd have been turned on more by the kind of people Cissy says you used to talk about in class, Malcolm. Doctors who gave themselves VD and yellow fever in the hope of finding a permanent cure."

"Well, it's taken us a while to learn to ride the dog," Malcolm said. "Let alone figure out how to teach it to ride the lizard."

Drawing the cork on another bottle, he added to himself, with a quizzical cock of one eyebrow, "Never could pour champagne without spilling it before I got VC . . . Val, you look kind of blank. You weren't at the council meeting at my old place when I used that metaphor."

"No, but I think I caught on anyway," Valentine said. "Not the kind of thing you'd chance across in my line—after all, I never got into psychology much, learned more about electronics and then later went for politics and economics . . . But I guess you're referring to three levels in the brain."

"Mm-hm. The trammels left over from earlier stages of evolution."

"Makes sense," Valentine said. "And that's what's going to change the world, isn't it? Catching on quick! Used to be that if you wanted to make somebody see things your way, you had to argue and persuade and *hammer* away. After VC—well, Wilfred and Arthur could tell you how to make the substrate they'd invented, and you could tell me, and the first time I tried it I got it right." He grinned broadly. "No sweat!"

"Before VC," Cissy put in, "you couldn't boil a potato!"

Joining the group with his glass empty and holding it up for replenishment, Bradshaw said, "What I think is going to change the world is our long overdue acceptance of the true nature of freedom. First you do what has to be done, and only then what you feel like doing. Ever since we evolved to consciousness we've been doing what we feel like doing and constantly losing our tempers when what ought to have been done because it had to be done interfered. I was talking to Hector just now"—pointing to the other end of the room, where Hector was leafing through a book found in Maurice's library—"about his patients, and he says he can see the impact of VC already. Because people now describe their symptoms more accurately he's treating twice as many of them in the same period of time and probably more effectively too."

"Delete that 'probably'," Hector said in a voice just loud enough to cut through the general chatter, continuing to flip through the book that had caught his eye . . . or rather, read it. For someone who had taken VC, as he had done a week ago, a single glance per page was enough.

—Something to do with being properly prepared psychologically. The sooner we can make the news of what's going on public, the better.

Malcolm sipped his champagne and over the glass gave Ruth a broad grin.

"There's one thing I can't reconcile myself to," she said. "Dalessandro being regarded as a great man. He's nothing but —but an arrogant dictator!"

"Oh, I think you do him an injustice," Malcolm murmured. "He was at least a patriot, genuinely concerned about the mess his country had been allowed to drift into, even though he was no better qualified to put it right than the people he was so rude about . . . that is, until Bob issued him a dose of VC. After which anyone who'd taken the trouble to keep reasonably well informed could have seen what was wrong with the EEC setup. He merely happened to be the first who was able to suggest improvements knowing that other people would listen because they'd just realised that they were likely to be blown up if they didn't."

"What's more it's a beautifully logical scheme," Sawyer put in. "One suspects that his military training contributed to it. Right, Bob?"

"I'm sure of it," Bradshaw said. "Malcolm is glad there's still room for sentiment in the world, and so am I. I'm glad that people like my friend who commands a Poseidon sub haven't entirely wasted their lives. Principles of strategy don't have to apply to warfare alone; they can be generalised, and Dalessandro has demonstrated the fact. Any competent officer could explain that if you want a body of men to behave well, you can be tough with them, but you must never under any circumstances be unfair or inconsistent. That's been the bane of our system, hasn't it? So few people rolling in more luxury than they knew what to do with, so many sweating their guts out and never earning a decent living . . . Thanks, of course, to the contradictory teachings of my former faith."

"I was brought up a Christian," Cissy said. "Spelt K-I-L-L-J-O-Y. My mam still is one. When I said I was going to quit the church because of what I'd learned from Val about the history of slavery, I thought she was going to kill *mel!*" She laughed nervously. But obviously that was not a joke.

"Yes, I predict that disillusionment is going to reach landslide proportions," Bradshaw said. "You see the Moral Polluters only quarter-filled Wembley Stadium for the climax of the New Year's Crusade? They were expecting ninety per cent capacity. Amelia Washgrave told me so herself."

"That's a reformed character, if you like," Cissy said. "And to think Toussaint and I did it when we took her those candies . . . !"

"She's recanted," Malcolm said. "But the one I'm waiting for is Charkall-Phelps. Maybe he never grew a conscience at all. Maybe he stifled it with his greed for power . . . That's a question for your theological chums, though, Bob." He hesitated. "By the way, you must be relieved that the part of your life you spent studying the subject can't be regarded as a total waste."

"I've been wondering about that," Kneller said. "Bob, how do you feel?"

"No, it wasn't wasted. Nothing's wasted. Nothing ever need be wasted, either past or future. Not now." Bradshaw sipped his wine. "You see . . . Well, we've been talking in metaphors about human personality, so I see no reason not to do the same about human community. I'd term the religious phase of our social evolution an adolescent phase, the logical sequel to the puerile phase in which, as we know, primitive people were unaware of the forces affecting their lives. Like children able to observe, and sometimes imitate, but never grasp the motives behind, the actions of their elders."

"To be followed by an adult stage?" Randolph suggested cynically.

"Well, at least an age in which we can begin to make up our own minds," Bradshaw said. "Free of the pubertal conflict between what we've been told is right and what our innate urges drive us to do. Time after time whole societies have become criminally insane, haven't they? Nazi Germany, New England at the time of the witch-hunts, countless others. But VC is going to change all that."

Ruth said with a visible shiver, "Is there anything it isn't going to change?"

"Nothing," Malcolm said positively. "Knowing what I used to know, I'd have guessed that its effects would take a long, long time to filter from the private to the public level. I'd have been overlooking something transcendentally obvious."

"One man in the right place at the right time," Kneller offered.

"Precisely. Maurice Post above all. Dalessandro too, in his way—after Bob's neat coup at the church in Arcovado."

"You mean the sewer bit?" Bradshaw chuckled. "I spotted that the moment I stepped off the train!"

"So you should add one thing in the right place at the right time," Randolph said.

"And our definition of 'right' has been revolutionised," Malcolm said, nodding. "*A priori* I'd have expected the relatively minor consequences, like greater empathy, greater sociability, touching the public scale only indirectly, for example by reducing racial tension." With a glance at Valentine and Cissy, "The sort of thing you told me happened to that sergeant in Glasgow, Val."

"Whereas what happened to his officer," Valentine said, "Lieutenant Cordery, who never actually came to my tea-van but always had his cuppa fetched for him, was far more significant. Seems that of all the things that could have happened to a soldier under his command nothing could have shaken him more than castration. Even before he caught VC what happened to poor Corporal Stevens caused him to start thinking through what he'd been told and comparing it with his actual experience. You know he's joined up with the strikers? He signed a communiqué on their behalf today."

"And a very reasonable set of proposals it contains," Hector said, joining them for the regular reason, an empty glass. "I hope it's going to succeed. I was so afraid I'd live to see my home town turn into a smoking pile of rubble like Belfast!"

"It would have done," Malcolm said, poising the bottle. "Not to mention London, Paris, Rome, New York, Moscow . . . Enjoying yourself, by the way?"

"I was never at a party I enjoyed more," Hector said with feeling. "Incidentally, I can name one thing that VC won't change in a hurry."

"Hmm?" Malcolm blinked at him. "It's revolutionising politics, economics and the arts; it's abolishing warfare; it's caused a painful reassessment of our attitudes to race and reproduction . . . Ah. You mean parties. And by extension the use of soft drugs."

"They'll last for a good few generations, at any rate," Hector said. "Hasn't part of our problem always been that while we could conceive ideal societies in imagination we've been surrounded by proof that we didn't inhabit a rationally organised world? Well, that'll change in the end, but probably not for a century."

"I don't know," Kneller objected. "This conference that's been called to rethink the Common Market and its relationship with poor countries from the bottom up: I'm sure it'll be the first such conference to produce concrete results."

"And the law's certain to be reviewed," Sawyer said. "The whole clumsy top-heavy system which has made it a dinosaur in most people's eyes, an anonymous impersonal expensive barrier between themselves and justice!"

"Granted, granted," Hector said. "What's more the politicians who got to the top by graft and glibness won't be able to fool people as they used to, and into the bargain they may grow consciences that wouldn't let them try! But when it comes to reforming the life-style of more than three thousand million people, all suddenly more individual than ever before . . . ! No, we're going to have to digest our heritage of irrationality, and that will be a very slow process."

With deliberate noisiness he gulped the rest of his wine and added, "Which means that we'll be swinking Posts for the foreseeable future."

"And vast," Malcolm said.

"Naturally!"

"Hmm! How interesting! It's started already, hasn't it? The change in language, I mean. Words are condensing. Were you aware, as a matter of curiosity, what you said just now?"

"Me?" Hector put his hand on his chest. "I . . . Oh, yes. I get it. No, I wasn't aware at the moment I said it that I'd packed *swinking for Post* and *drinking a toast* together. But . . . Well, did anyone miss the point?"

"Not except for Toussaint, I imagine," Malcolm murmured. "Who would hardly have read any Middle English, at his age . . . It's happened to me once or twice, too. It feels from the inside a bit like stammering in reverse. It's the listener who's slow to react, not the speaker. But we'll adjust. When I think how much more action we shall be able to cram into a given time, how much more communication into fewer words . . . It's going to be a fascinating world. Painful, but the pains will be growing-pains. He among us who was within sight posted the first stone and it won't come down."

As he spoke, everybody's attention had fixed on him, and now everybody laughed except Toussaint, who looked puzzled, and—to Malcolm's surprise—Kneller, who said, "What?"

"You don't get the reference? Ah, perhaps you never took an interest in folk-tales."

"No, I have to admit I never did."

"You should know this one. After all, you're among the handful of people who have stoned the entire world. It's my favourite Jack the Giant Killer story. Jack left home to seek his fortune carrying nothing but a bag, a cheese his mother had made, and a bird he had caught. On his way he met a giant. The giant swore to gobble him up if he couldn't match him in a trial of strength, and first he picked up a rock and crushed it so hard that water oozed out. So Jack squeezed the cheese and the whey ran out. Then the giant threw a stone clear out of sight, and it was a long, long time before it fell back. So Jack pretended the bird was a pebble, and of course it flew away. His stone never came down.

"Disgusted at being unable to defeat this weakling, the giant took Jack home for supper and challenged him to an eating contest. Jack poured all the porridge he was given down the bag he had hidden under his coat, and in trying to keep up with him the giant overate and died of a surfeit. So Jack inherited the giant's castle and—"

"Lived happily ever after!" Toussaint shouted, jumping off Cissy's knee.

"I hope so," Malcolm said. "A chance like this won't happen twice. Killing is easy. Living with is not."

Toussaint blinked and his mouth fell ajar.

"Never mind, son," Malcolm said, rumpling his black hair. "You'll catch on."

"You won't be able to *help* catching on," said Valentine.

NEL

21

YEARS

BESTSELLERS

T035 794	HOW GREEN WAS MY VALLEY	Richard Llewellyn	95p
T039 560	I BOUGHT A MOUNTAIN	Thomas Firbank	90p
T033 988	IN TEETH OF THE EVIDENCE	Dorothy L. Sayers	90p
T040 755	THE KING MUST DIE	Macy Renault	85p
T038 149	THE CARPETBAGGERS	Harold Robbins	£1.50
T040 917	TO SIR WITH LOVE	E. R. Braithwaite	75p
T041 719	HOW TO LIVE WITH A NEUROTIC DOG	Stephen Baker	75p
T040 925	THE PRIZE	Irving Wallace	£1.60
T034 755	THE CITADEL	A. J. Cronin	£1.10
T034 674	STRANGER IN STRANGE LAND	Robert Heinlein	£1.20
T037 673	BABY & CHILD CARE	Dr Benjamin Spock	£1.50
T037 053	79 PARK AVENUE	Harold Robbins	£1.25
T035 697	DUNE	Frank Herbert	£1.25
T035 832	THE MOON IS A HARSH MISTRESS	Robert Heinlein	£1.00
T040 933	THE SEVEN MINUTES	Irving Wallace	£1.50
T038 130	THE INHERITORS	Harold Robbins	£1.25
T035 689	RICH MAN POOR MAN	Irvin Shaw	£1.50
T037 134	EDGE 27: DEATH DRIVE	George Gilman	75p
T037 541	DEVIL'S GUARD	Robert Elford	£1.25
T038 386	THE RATS	James Herbert	75p
T030 342	CARRIE	Stephen King	75p
T033 759	THE FOG	James Herbert	80p
T033 740	THE MIXED BLESSING	Helen von Slyke	£1.25
T037 061	BLOOD AND MONEY	Thomas Thomson	£1.50

NEL P.O. BOX 11, FALMOUTH TR10 9EN, CORNWALL.

U.K. Customers: Please allow 22p for the first book plus 10p per copy for each additional book ordered to a maximum charge of 82p.

B.F.P.O. & Eire: Please allow 22p for the first book plus 10p per copy for the next 6 books thereafter 4p per book.

Overseas Customers: Please allow 30p for the first book plus 10p per copy for each additional book.

Name ....

Address ....

....

Title ....

While every effort is made to keep prices low, it is sometimes necessary to increase prices at short notice. New English Library reserve the right to show on covers and charge new retail prices which may differ from those advertised in the text or elsewhere.